Jerusha is afraid to let Keith love her.

"I can see it's a good thing I came out tonight," he offered quietly.

For the first time during the evening, she looked him straight in the eyes. "Why?"

"I thought our conversation last night might have left you uncomfortable. You don't have to be embarrassed at letting me see the person you are inside, Jerusha. I think you're pretty special, and I'm honored you'd trust me with what you think."

She shrugged, wishing she could regain her previous detachment. Emotions didn't get embarrassing when she kept her distance.

"I mean it, Rushi."

His use of David's nickname and his hand on her shoulder unsettled her too much. She jerked away.

"Hey!" His voice dropped almost to a whisper. "What is it?"

She backed further from him. "I wish you wouldn't touch me." She could feel his gaze on her face, though she concentrated on pouring gravy into the dish of potatoes.

"Jerusha, please look at me." The pleading in his voice reached her more intimately than a physical touch. "Please don't feel upset over last night. It's not weakness to need comfort. You're dealing with a lot of pain, and I believe God invented hugs to get us through those hard times. I'm glad I was the one He chose to help you."

JANELLE BURNHAM is fast becoming one of **Heartsong Presents'** most popular authors. Janelle is from British Columbia, Canada, and has been writing for over ten years.

Books by Janelle Burnham

HEARTSONG PRESENTS

HP53—Midnight Music
HP100—River of Peace
HP119—Beckoning Streams

Winding Highway

Janelle Burnham

Stories of Peace

Heartsong Presents

To Phyllis Pettigrew:

- *with whom I've dreamed, cried, laughed, and prayed.*
- *whose path has taken unpredictable turns but whose faith remains a beacon for mine.*

A note from the Author:
I love to hear from my readers! You may write to me at the following address:

Janelle Burnham
Author Relations
P.O. Box 719
Uhrichsville, OH 44683

ISBN 1-55748-763-4

WINDING HIGHWAY

Cover illustration by Kathy Arbuckle.

PRINTED IN THE U.S.A.

one

For the umpteenth time in less than an hour, Jerusha Porter stirred vegetables bubbling in a stew pot and checked baking powder biscuits in the bread warmer near the stovepipe. Her brother could be so exasperatingly concerned about others, even to the detriment of his own health and home life! He had seen a firelike glow coming from Stein's warehouse six blocks away in the downtown area of frontier Dawson Creek, and even though she had just started serving up supper, he had insisted on "going to see if I can help."

His patient, gentle explanation didn't ease her irritation. "That building used to be livery stable, so the upper storey is full of hay. If it's really on fire, the boys are going to need help getting it out."

"The boys!" she muttered derisively, pushing a couple of loose bobby pins more firmly into the twist of black hair at the back of her head. No matter how hard she tried, she couldn't think of the ever-present American army troops as anything but heathens. David, on the other hand, seemed determined to be a personal friend to each of the thousands of soldiers camped on the hill beside Dawson Creek. *This isn't the only area of contrast in our ideas about ministry*, she reminded herself.

"The ministry" had been a prominent concept in both their lives as far back as she could remember. Their parents, Nathan and Mary Porter, had met each other on a mission station in Kenya, and David and Jerusha had been born there. When Jerusha was ten and David, eleven, the family had returned to Winnipeg on furlough and the children had been enrolled in a local school. Their parents departed for a new mission assignment only six months later, leaving David and Jerusha in the care of Mary's sister and brother-in-law, Cameron and Vivienne McDonald. Jerusha could count on the fingers of one hand the number of times she'd seen her parents since. Though they returned to Canada for year-long furloughs every four years, some crisis always sent them back to "the field" after a mere month or two.

Peering out the kitchen window, Jerusha could see men and vehicles moving quickly toward the center of town. For once she felt grateful their parsonage and newly constructed church hovered on the edge of the equally new Alaska Highway. She would be able to keep track of what was happening as effectively as the crowds now streaming in the direction of the warehouse. *Fools!! Why would they want to bundle up against subzero temperatures just to watch a fire being extinguished?* The glow of the fire lit the early evening darkness so she could see trees bending in the wind. What an uncivilized country! As if forty-below- zero weren't enough, the wind never stopped blowing.

A thundering boom assaulted Jerusha's eardrums. Then the parsonage shuddered as if struck by a gigantic hand. Suddenly she wanted to be outside. Where was David? How could she help him if she didn't know where to find him? A siren screamed not far away, then another joined it. Even from her vantage point of relative distance, she could see the fire had spread. Another shock wave, smaller this time, shook the building. What was happening? Knowing her brother, she figured he had probably charged into the middle of the disaster. What would she do if he were injured?

At least she'd have a valid reason for returning to Winnipeg. Answering the call to pastor in Dawson Creek had been David's idea. His face had glowed as he'd shown her the letter his Bible College dean had given him. "It's from a group of about a dozen families who've been an informal fellowship for about fifteen years. They feel they're now able to support a full-time, formally trained pastor, so they're asking the College to recommend a graduate. Dean Pauley said he thought immediately of me. What an opportunity!"

Much as she loved her aunt and uncle, she couldn't bear the thought of being separated from her brother. Besides, it wouldn't do for her to be the only member of the Porter family not involved in The Ministry. She'd volunteered to accompany him as housekeeper and parsonage hostess. How often in the past six months had she wished for the opportunity to choose again! Their parents' example didn't obligate Jerusha to follow her brother to the end of the earth, did it? She'd often wondered what her life would have been like had Mary Porter chosen motherhood over the mission field. Uncle Cam and Aunt Vivienne had been wonderful guardians, but Jerusha still had to force aside resentment at her parents' absence from her life. One of these days, God would surely punish her severely for not admiring their sacrifice as her aunt so verbally did. She wondered what her mother would think of this boom town at the end of the rail line, its population swelling daily even in the grip of mid-winter. Of course, what would be left when the men finally gained control of the fire? Maybe the destruction would be severe enough to push David back to civilization.

Not a chance. Jerusha felt her lips tighten in frustration. For some reason, David loved this town with its overabundance of military personnel, its fortune-seeking opportunists, and its slow-moving farmers. Should fire reduce the buildings to rubble, he'd feel invigorated by the challenge of rebuilding. She mentally pictured his blue eyes sparkling with excitement, his black hair standing on end from his absent-minded rumpling, and his tall, lanky body bent forward as if he couldn't get to his destination quickly enough. What if fire destroyed the church and parsonage he'd built practically single-handedly? He'd probably say something ridiculous like, "The Lord gives and the Lord takes away," and start planning a new building. She really should plan how to rescue their few belongings if the fire spread this far. Looking around the sitting room, she evaluated what should be preserved. A cloth-covered bench along one wall caught her attention. The steamer trunk she'd covered to make a seat for David's ever-present visitors. It would make perfect storage and protection. She dragged the trunk to David's study corner and quickly piled his books into it. Then she hurried up the ladder to his loft-bedroom to collect his one good suit and his work clothes. Next, she went to her bedroom for her Sunday frock and her three day dresses, gathered her aprons from the kitchen, and took the bedding from the shelves by her room. Cooking utensils could be stuffed into the burlap grain bag by the back porch. She reached for the bag as the back door shook from heavy blows. Should she open it or pretend not to be home?

The blows came again, this time sounding as though the door were being kicked, while a heavily-accented voice called, “Open up, ma’am. I’ve got the reverend here. He’s been hurt. I can’t help ’til I put him down.”

With a gasp, Jerusha jerked the door open to admit a soldier in a blood-covered uniform and crookedly placed combat helmet. Used to her brother’s skinny height, she noticed immediately this man’s relative shortness. In fact, he stood only a few inches taller than her own five foot three. A red cross on a white square emblazoned on the helmet’s center announced his medical knowledge. Blood oozed from a horrible-looking bump on David’s head, which lolled off one of the medic’s arms. His legs dangled off the other, one of them at an awkward angle.

“He’ll be all right, ma’am, but I have to lay him somewhere.” The soldier spoke reassuringly, yet with authority.

Jerusha tried to focus her thoughts. There would be no way the soldier could carry David up the ladder to his own room, nor would it be easy for her to care for him up there. Yet she didn’t want him in the sitting room where visitors could disturb him at all hours.

“Let’s put him in here.” She led the way to her own room, flipping the electric wall switch to light the room and swiftly pulling down the blanket covering her bed.

“Do you have an extra sheet?” The soldier didn’t relinquish his burden.

Jerusha nodded, wishing he’d just hurry and fix David.

“Fold it in half width-wise and lay it in the middle of the bed. I’ll put the reverend on top of it, so we don’t have to change all the bedding when I get him fixed up. He’s your brother?”

She answered his question aloud while she grabbed two

sheets from the trunk. She and David looked enough alike to be twins, so the American's observation came as no surprise. Did he really know what to do for David, or was he just acting? She folded the two sheets and laid them end to end on the bed.

"Thanks, ma'am." The soldier set David down gently. "I also need hot water, clean rags, and fresh clothes for him."

Jerusha hurried to the kitchen stove, where she dipped steaming water from the built-in boiler into a metal washpan, then rummaged through her rag bag for a couple of soft cloths. She delivered the items, then scampered up to David's room for his pajamas. Somehow she hadn't thought about packing them. What if they still had to escape from the fire? How would she move him?

"David told me to be prepared for evacuation if the fire came this way," she said when she re-entered what had become the sickroom. "How am I going to get him out?"

"I don't think you'll have to, ma'am." The soldier lifted his gaze from his quick moving hands to direct another reassuring smile at her. "Everything seems under control at this point." He bent back over his patient, giving her a clear view of wide, well-muscled shoulders. His stockiness emphasized the gentleness with which he attended David.

Silence hovered while Jerusha watched him wipe soot, blood, and dirt from David's face. Her brother remained unconscious. How soon would he wake up, or would he? She suddenly felt the need to touch him. Only his leg was close enough for her to reach without getting in the way. The movement attracted the soldier's gaze.

"He'll wake up soon enough. Something hit him on the

head hard enough to knock him out, and I hope he stays out until I get that leg set. Could I trouble you for his razor? I'd like to shave a little of his hair away from this bump so I can make sure it's clean."

Glad to have something to do, Jerusha went in search of the razor. When she came back, David's shirt was off and his rescuer had another request. "Do you have anything to make cloth strips from?" He pulled the bed away from the wall into the center of the small room.

She thought for a moment. "The Winnipeg Ladies' Aid sent us some worn-out sheets in our most recent missionary barrel. Would that work?"

"Perfect. Could you tear them the long way into four-inch strips, and I'll call when I'm ready for them." He smiled again before turning his attention back to David.

The barrel stood in a corner of the kitchen where David had put it yesterday. Thankfully, the lid was still loose, and the sheets near the top. She quickly ripped them as instructed, realizing how tactfully she'd been banished from the sickroom while the soldier changed David's clothes. She wished she could think of a tactful way to find out the stranger's name. In less time than seemed possible, she heard him call, "I'm ready for the bandages whenever you can bring them."

David had begun to stir and the soldier's relaxed manner vanished. "We don't have long before he comes to. Can you quickly find me something to use for a splint?"

"There are a few boards left over from the church benches David made this morning. Would they work?"

"They should, at least until we can find something better if we need it. Where are they?"

Jerusha led the way through a door in the sitting room to

the meeting area. Turning on the lights revealed an array of building supplies littering the floor. It only took the soldier a couple of moments to find what he needed.

"These are perfect." He picked up two narrow pieces and a third wider one. "In fact, more than I'd hoped for. Can I get you to hold him still while I work? If he's waking up, he may fight back when I grab that leg."

David moaned when they entered the room. "I'm not sure I'll be much help," Jerusha admitted, looking at her brother's thrashing frame.

"I've learned a bit about controlling these big dudes. Size isn't everything, you know." The soldier grinned and showed Jerusha how to brace herself against the bed, then hold her arms across David's body to still him. He pulled on the broken leg. David struggled, then abruptly went limp.

"Good. He's out again. Would you please hand me a couple of cloth strips?" He wound the material snugly around David's leg, then positioned the wider board underneath with the narrower boards on the sides. "Hopefully these bandages will keep the leg from chafing against the wood. Now for more strips to secure the splints." He worked quickly and confidently. "You'll probably have to cut off one leg of his pajama bottoms to get them over the splint, but he shouldn't have any trouble with his underclothes. Now for that bump on his head." He folded one of the strips to form a pad that he held in place with another strip wrapped around David's head. A couple more strips finished the bandage. "I'll turn him on his side if you'll fold the extra sheets toward him. Good. Now we'll change sides, and I'll roll him the other way and you can pull them out from under him. Easy as sliding off the road, wouldn't you say?" He grinned, once again relaxed.

"What do I do with him now?" Jerusha couldn't imagine how to care for her brother without help. She'd never felt so helpless, so frustrated.

"He'll sleep for a while, probably until tomorrow some time. For the first couple of days, he'll be pretty quiet while he recovers from the head blow. After that, the hard part will be keeping him still long enough for the leg to heal. I'll try to check on him at least once a day, and I'll see if I can bring something in case the pain gets to bothering him."

"Are you a doctor?" The question popped out before Jerusha could think about its propriety.

A pair of eyes as blue as David's twinkled when he grinned again. "Sorry I haven't introduced myself. I'm Corporal Keith Sutherland, U.S. Army Medic, at your service, ma'am." He swept his combat helmet off in an elaborate bow, revealing a blond crew cut.

"Pleased to meet you." Jerusha didn't know how to respond to his breezy humor. "I'm Jerusha Porter. How did you know where to bring David?"

"He visits us army boys often, as I'm sure you know, and made sure we're all aware of where he lives in case we want to drop by."

"How did he get hurt?" She blinked away threatening tears.

"The warehouse had dynamite and percussion caps stored in it. The fire set it all off, which sent the downtown area flying. You've never seen a mess like we've got over there now. I hate to rush off, ma'am, but I've got to get back. I'll check in again tomorrow." Another bright grin, a wave, several quick thumps of his boots, and he was gone into the fire-lit night.

two

Jerusha felt silence close in behind Corporal Sutherland's departure. Then commotion from downtown overwhelmed it—more sirens screaming, army trucks roaring, people yelling, and it seemed she could hear the fire crackling. She noticed wet spots left by snow melting off the soldier's boots onto the wood plank floor, and black smudges where soot had rubbed off. What to do next? Weariness suddenly made her limbs feel heavy, though her mind still raced. The clock showed only thirty minutes past eight. She should at least get the stew into a bowl to stay cold in the back entry area that served as mudroom, storage room, and cold room. Maybe egg gravy for breakfast would make the biscuits edible. She'd wait until morning to unpack the trunk...just in case. Where should she sleep? David rested quietly in her bed. She could use his bed, but she might not hear him if he awoke, and the ladder would make getting to him quickly difficult. Maybe a pallet on the floor in the sitting room would be the best idea. Thank goodness the Winnipeg Ladies' Aid had seemed to believe bedding to be their most pressing need. Jerusha had laughed derisively when David had first opened the barrel to reveal blankets and sheets in abundance.

"They must think we're running a hospital, not starting a church," she had grumbled, recalling the bedding showered on them before they left. "Too bad all these sheets couldn't make me a house dress or a new shirt for you."

"Don't fret, Rushi." David laughed with genuine amusement. "I know it's frustrating to feel our people back home don't understand what we're doing here, but God never sends us anything we don't need. I'll keep this lid on loosely, and we'll wait to see what He has in mind for His bed clothes."

With a small amount of gratitude, Jerusha now extracted enough blankets to make a soft pad, then a couple of sheets and another three blankets to keep herself warm on the cold floor. She'd have to make sure she stoked the fire well, both in the barrel stove and in the cookstove. Not only did they need extra warmth in this frigid weather, but she wasn't sure she could start the fires again should they go out. She filled each stove with as much wood as it could hold, then pulled the dampers shut to keep the wood from burning too quickly.

Too tense for sleep, she decided to indulge in a quick sponge bath and a cup of warm milk before bed. She turned out all the lights in the house so she wouldn't be visible through the curtains, dumped her soiled dress onto the pile of David's clothing left by the medic, and pulled her flannel gown and wrapper from their pegs beside the door. Though the damp cloth on her skin caused her to shiver, the feeling of cleanliness combined with the cozy warmth of her nightgown did bring relaxation. She thought about turning a light back on before she dumped the soiled water, but decided against it. The sky's red glow lent enough light that she wouldn't bump into things, and the semi-darkness was soothing. She tiptoed into the sickroom for the pan of water used by the medic, then carried it and her own washpan to the back door and flung their contents across the snow. Theoretically, their house was tied into the city drainage system, but she knew from experience how unreliable the system was. When the water drained at all, it went down so slowly as to leave her sink unusable for at least half an hour. As it was, dirty water from the pipes often bubbled up through her drain to fill the sink. She'd never had the sink overflow, but she knew it would happen some day. Just one more problem in this town that had mushroomed from seven hundred people to more than four thousand civilians in less than a year.

She wondered again what had drawn so many people to this desolate place. For some reason she had yet to discover, the U.S. Army had decided to build a highway from Dawson Creek, British Columbia, to Fairbanks, Alaska, as part of the war effort. Locals were outspoken in their disdain of what they saw as an impossible project, which seemed totally unrelated to the carnage in Europe. Some even went so far as to declare that the men and money being utilized in highway building could be much more effectively used where the war was actually taking place.

However, construction had brought prosperity of sorts to what had been simply a frontier village. With Dawson Creek being the northern terminus of the railway, all army and construction supplies and personnel were funnelled through the tiny community. Carpenters, truckers, laborers, and opportunists from all over had come to join the action. The army paid their contractors well, and those who couldn't get work for the army directly could easily make a living at the myriad of services needed by the mushrooming boom town. One of David's parishioners, a white-haired woman named Mrs. Barry, had doubled the size of her boardinghouse and said she had every room filled every night. Sometimes she and her niece, Maisie, even had to double up in her room to provide more space for guests. Jerusha couldn't imagine allowing those uncouth types into the house, much less cooking and cleaning for them, too. She shuddered at the thought.

Back in the kitchen, she scooped two tablespoons of milk powder into a cup and added a tablespoon of honey. Here was another symbol of this uncivilized place. Who could possibly be fooled into thinking this powder mixed with water would replace real milk? Six months ago, she hadn't been able to tolerate its taste. Unfortunately, the farms around this community couldn't keep up with the demand for milk, butter, and cheese. Such products could be brought in by train, but were too expensive for the Porters' budget. So she had learned to first accept, then even enjoy, the powdered milk beverage, as long as it was hot. She wrapped her hands around the warm cup, wishing it had been that easy to adapt to other changes in her lifestyle.

For one thing, money had become almost nonexistent. Having grown up in relative comfort due to Uncle Cam's successful business ventures, Jerusha found herself continually frustrated by David's limited and irregular salary. Over the winter, his pay had often come in the form of food and firewood. Even so, she'd been forced to take in laundry from the boardinghouse to earn necessary income. Though the job only included bedding, she still felt demeaned.

She pulled the pins from her hair. Mother and Aunt Vivienne had never cut their hair, so neither had Jerusha. Her fine, thin strands refused to style as gracefully as theirs, but cutting it would be giving in to worldliness. As she brushed, she felt it catch on the roughness of her fingers. Her hands had once been her single private vanity. Days of lifting sheets from soapy water and hanging them outside in stinging wind had reddened and cracked them. Their condition both mortified and continually reminded her of what she'd given up to remain at her brother's side. As she inched into her makeshift bed, she wished yet again he'd just give up and take her back where she belonged.

It seemed she had only slept a few moments when she heard a knock at the back door. Who could it be at this time of night? If it were someone with evil intent, they wouldn't bother knocking. She belted her wrapper snugly around her and hurried to the entry. Before she could inquire, a somewhat familiar voice called, "It's Corporal Sutherland, Miss Porter. May I talk to you about something urgent?"

With a small sigh of relief, she switched on a light and opened the door. "Come in."

"Sorry to disturb you so late, or should I say so early. It's this way, Miss Porter. The hospital is full up with people injured when the dynamite blew. It's against regulation to bring civilians into the army hospital, and we still have wounded lying on the boardwalks and in the streets closed off from traffic. I noticed your meeting room is fairly large as well as being close by. Would it be possible for us to use it? An army team will take care of the medical end of things if we can just get the patients out of the cold."

She didn't have to wonder what David would say. He wouldn't hesitate. Besides, the barrel in the corner of the kitchen still contained innumerable blankets and sheets. Could this be why it had been sent? In any case, no good minister or his family ever refused to be helpful.

Corporal Sutherland sensed her hesitation. "I doubt we'll be noisy enough to disturb the reverend. In fact, it will keep me close by in case he needs help." Another charming grin erased some of the weariness etched around his eyes.

"I'm sure my brother would be delighted to make the room available. The front doors are unlocked. Shall I make up beds on the floor or on the benches?"

"Maybe we'll push three benches together for treatment areas, and pallets on the floor for sleeping patients. I wish we could bring cots over from the infirmary, but the trucks wouldn't be able to get through the mess downtown. God bless you, Miss Porter. We'll be back shortly." He lifted his combat helmet and vanished again.

Jerusha hurried to the meeting room, where she quickly stacked the short pieces of lumber against one wall. The long pieces were too difficult to lift without entangling her long gown. She hoped she could get the area cleared to her satisfaction before the men showed up. It wouldn't do for the reverend's sister to be seen in her nightclothes in the company of soldiers. She decided to unload the blankets and sheets from the barrel, then go change. The church would be turned into a hospital, so she, the minister's sister, would have to be on hand to help.

She'd just pulled on a dress when thumps from the meeting area announced the beginning of the rescue effort. She quickly fastened the last buttons on her dress, tied on a white apron, and hurried into the makeshift first aid station. Two soldiers had already begun carrying lumber outside, and another two, wearing helmets that matched Corporal Sutherland's, were pushing benches together, padding each "bed" with a blanket, and covering each with a carefully folded sheet. One of the medics looked up as she entered.

"Hello, ma'am. The corporal said to thank you again for your generosity."

Smiling her acknowledgement, Jerusha reached for a blanket with which to make up a floor pallet. The gratitude made her feel guilty, since the offer hadn't been her idea or even her choice. She'd simply done what any good minister's sister would do, regardless of her personal feelings. Familiar resentment churned inside as she worked. Unbidden, she mentally heard her aunt's voice praising her mother's dedication. She reminded herself that she wasn't doing this only for David, but also for her family's reputation. She couldn't belittle her parents' sacrifice by cringing from her duty. The thought didn't change how she felt about the hardships of this town, the rough company, and now being forced into nursing duty simply because she was David's sister.

"Miss Porter." Corporal Sutherland's voice broke into her introspection.

She looked up, unaware he'd come in.

He stood beside a makeshift bed, a thrashing child in his arms. "Would you help me soothe this young man? I can't do much for him until we get him quiet."

His apparent confidence in her ability warred against the nervousness she always felt around children. "I don't know how much good I'll do." She stood slowly, rubbing her hands in her apron.

"Kids usually respond better to women. All we can do for any of these people is try." He smiled encouragingly and put the child on the bed.

Jerusha instinctively reached for the boy's hands while murmuring whatever came to mind. "Calm down, young man. We can't help you if you won't let us. That's it. Lie still, now. It won't hurt as badly if you don't move." To her surprise, the thrashing stopped.

"Looks like you have the touch, Miss Porter. Keep it up, and I'll have him bandaged in no time."

She never knew what kept her going until the first rays of sunshine created a murky dawn through the heavy smoke still blanketing the town. It seemed the procession of injured people would never end. Head wounds, broken bones, unconscious people without visible injuries, and cuts and scrapes in abundance. Corporal Sutherland's unending gentle humor and continuing energy amazed her. He seemed genuinely contented and appeared to want to help these people. She wished she could feel that "want to." It would be so much easier to be the proper minister's sister if she had the emotions to go along with the part.

"I think that does it for now." Corporal Sutherland motioned for another medic to help him lift a patient with a sprained ankle to one of the last three pallets. "Shall I look in on the reverend before I report back to the base?"

"Yes, please." Jerusha felt like she'd been run over by a truck and hoped fervently no one would decide to visit until she'd been able to grab some sleep. But then who would keep watch over the wounded who littered the church? She sighed wearily, ignoring memories of her luxurious bed and quiet, spacious room in Winnipeg.

"I'll see if I can get a couple of my men assigned to our little first aid station here so you can catch some rest. I'm sorry we've imposed on you so severely." Concern showed past the exhaustion imprinted on his face.

"The church isn't much good unless it's used for more than social gatherings," Jerusha replied automatically, quoting one of David's favorite sayings.

"It's too bad more people don't believe that." Corporal Sutherland followed his comment with enigmatic silence. Jerusha wondered if he saw through her act of dedication. She shook her head, trying to clear the guilt. She was just tired. What would he care, so long as she helped? He was just one of those military heathen, anyway.

Corporal Sutherland placed a squarish hand on David's forehead at the edge of the bandage. "No fever, and he seems to be resting well. When he wakes up, he'll probably want to get up right away. If you can, keep him still and feed him as lightly as he'll allow. Porridge would be a good idea, or light soup. Make sure he doesn't try to walk on that leg."

"Thanks for the help, Corporal." Jerusha clutched the edge of the doorway to steady herself in a world that suddenly seemed to tilt and spin.

"Pleased to—Miss Porter!" She heard alarm in his voice and firm hands grabbed her arms just as she felt herself falling. "Here, sit down." He unceremoniously pushed her onto the bed and shoved her head between her knees.

The stench of unwashed bodies and stale blood in her apron threatened to overturn her stomach, though her head cleared. She straightened slowly, working to keep the room in focus. "I'm sorry. I'm not in the habit of fainting."

"Don't apologize, Miss Porter. Lack of sleep and food combined with a night of hard work will do that to anyone. Do you have some soup I can warm for you?"

Jerusha couldn't find the words to refuse him politely. "On the shelf in the back entry. It's frozen."

"I'll find it. Don't go to sleep on me. I'll be right back."

She felt far too light-headed to stand up. She forced herself to focus on David's face, then on the fire-tinged sky outside her window. It seemed only moments until the medic returned with a steaming bowl. "I'll hold it if you think you can handle the spoon." Again his smile encouraged her while he knelt on the floor.

Gradually, clear thinking returned while the soup's warmth spread throughout her body. She felt almost ready to handle the new day without sleep.

"If smell is any indication, you must be a pretty good cook," Corporal Sutherland observed.

Jerusha grinned at the obvious hint. "I must be some sort of beast to eat in front of you. Help yourself before you leave."

"Since I don't want to pass out getting back to camp, I'd better accept your offer." Humor twinkled from his exhaustion-ringed eyes.

They both stood, but a sound from the bed stopped their departure. "Rushi." The corporal lifted an eyebrow at Jerusha before stepping past her to David's side. Slowly, David's eyes opened. "Rushi?" He called again.

"Right here, David. How do you feel?" A dizzying feeling of relief weakened her knees again.

"What's with my leg? My head. I shouldn't be sleeping—"

The medic quickly interrupted what was turning into a restless tirade. "I think you should, Reverend. I found you under a couple of wooden beams near the Co-op store. You have a nasty bump on your head and a broken leg. Sleep's the best thing for you."

"Keith?" David seemed unsure of what he saw.

"That's me, Rev. The boss of this here temporary first aid station."

"May I eat?" David's buoyant good humor asserted

itself as he became more alert.

"If you'll promise to be quiet and absolutely no trouble to your sister. She's been up all night helping us in your meeting room, which we've turned into a recovery area."

"Thanks, Rushi." David's gentle gaze told her he realized the struggle she'd been though. His uncanny perception both reassured and intimidated her. He looked back to the medic. "If you can help me take care of a little personal problem, Corporal, I think I'll be able to rest a lot better."

Jerusha felt her cheeks flame as both men chuckled. "I'll have soup waiting for both of you when you're ready."

three

By Wednesday morning, the last of the invalids had been moved to the hospital or taken home. Dr. Pierce, a tall, smiling man and one of David's most faithful parishioners, stopped by the parsonage that evening.

"Sorry I couldn't come earlier, Miss Porter," he apologized. "Since Keith found him, I knew he'd been well taken care of, and I've been so busy my wife has almost forgotten what I look like." He grinned. "Keith wanted me to double-check his work, though."

"Thanks for coming." Jerusha directed him to the bedroom. This made the second time Jerusha had heard Corporal Sutherland referred to with respect. Generally, civilians held the army in distrust, and soldiers kept mostly to themselves. Somehow this medic had reached beyond the barriers to earn a rapport with civilians. He'd certainly gained her confidence. She yanked her thoughts back to the real doctor, whom she heard conversing with his patient in the sickroom.

"Couldn't have looked after him better myself," Dr. Pierce smiled when he came out. "Your brother's head wound is healing nicely. I would have liked to have set his leg in plaster, but we're fresh out. The reverend should be okay with the splints if you can keep him still. Good day, ma'am." He left chuckling at his own joke.

"Rushi." David's call brought Jerusha running. He had already pushed himself into a sitting position. Obviously, keeping still didn't rank high on his list of priorities.

"David!" She tried to keep her voice calm and rational.

"I'm being careful." His grin ruined the reassuring tone of his voice. "I just can't handle lying here any more. Keith brought me some crutches this morning, and I'd like to try them out before this evening's service."

The urge to shriek at him almost overpowered her. "You're still planning church for tonight?"

"Why not? The hard part will be getting to the meeting room. Nobody will mind if I don't stand at the pulpit, and you can help me prop my leg on a chair. But first, I need presentable clothes and some practice with the crutches."

Jerusha glared at him. "Why not just cancel the service?"

"Our people need encouragement." Laughter had disappeared from his eyes, replaced by a gentleness and something else she couldn't define.

"But they would understand if we cancelled just for tonight. Besides, they'll probably all be busy and won't come anyway." She tried to push him back onto the pillows, but he enveloped her hands in his own.

"They will come, Rushi. Disaster shows people how much they need each other, and God."

She tried to pull away. "They can find God at home. They functioned for years without you. There's no need to drag yourself out of bed."

"I'll be fine, little sister. I need them as much as they need me."

Jerusha brought his clothes, helped him dress, walked with him while he practiced with his crutches, then busied herself tidying up the meeting room while he slept, all the while contrasting his words with her feelings. She thought of this town as a mission field, its people as heathens, its

Christians as converts. How could he feel he needed them when he'd come to help them? She remembered his eyes as he'd spoken of them. Their expression certainly bore no resemblance to her own sense of duty.

To her surprise, their meeting room began to fill early. She noticed several people who hadn't attended before, as well as a few who usually came only for the Sunday service. David sat at the front of the room, his injured leg positioned on pillows on a chair in front of him. Each person who came went straight to him before finding a seat. Jerusha watched him carefully for signs of fatigue. Instead of becoming tired, though, he seemed more invigorated with each hand he shook. He inquired after the women's homes and families, ruffled the children's hair, and swapped stories with the men. Occasionally, his hearty laugh filled the room with joy. She wished she'd been able to clean more thoroughly, instead of just pushing the benches into place, moving the bedding to their own sitting room, and sweeping the floor.

"He loves these people, doesn't he?"

The deep voice near her ear caused Jerusha to jump. She turned to glare at its owner, but her gaze was met by a pair of sparkling blue eyes. "Corporal Sutherland!"

"At your service, ma'am." As he swept a low bow, she noticed his freshly pressed uniform, carefully knotted tie, and the cloth hat he held. His presence added to her discomfort.

"I'm sure the reverend will be pleased to see you here."

He sobered as he looked at her, but his eyes retained their twinkle. "A few of the guys in my outfit have the night off and decided they'd like to come here. Funny how disaster makes people think of God." He moved off toward David.

She stared after him. He'd echoed David's earlier comment. What made him and David so different from her? She sensed they truly loved the people around them. She cared about some of them, too, she defended herself, seeing Maisie Clarke follow Mrs. Barry through the doorway. She'd become acquainted with the plump young woman soon after arriving, and their friendship had grown mostly because Maisie refused to leave Jerusha to herself.

"Jerusha! I'm so glad you weren't hurt, too. How is the reverend?" Maisie's round face wore its usual sunny smile.

"He insisted on being here tonight, even though I think he should have stayed in bed."

"He probably needed to see his people." Maisie studied him for a moment. "I think we needed to see him, too."

"He said the same thing." Where had it come from—this mysterious bond between her brother and these strangers?

"And we have visitors tonight! Do you know who they are?" Bubbling interest turned Maisie's eyes to green twinkles.

"The shorter man is the medic who brought David home, but I don't know who the others are."

More familiar arrivals distracted Maisie from the strangers. "And here come Lewis and Sheila Murray! He doesn't often come into town on a week night."

The two women waited eagerly for the couple to come inside. Sheila formed a third in their trio of friendship, as equally determined to include Jerusha as Maisie.

"I'm so glad you came! How are you feeling?" Maisie studied Sheila carefully, though her friend's small frame had yet to make her pregnancy visible.

"Jist fine, and that's the truth of it." Sheila smiled as

easily as Maisie, her Irish brogue thickening as she talked. "And how is it you are, Jerusha? Lewis told me you were in the thick of it t'other night."

"We just did what needed to be done." Jerusha felt uncomfortable under her friends' scrutiny. "At least the bedding in the missionary barrel came in handy."

"Lewis will be coming to town tomorrow. How about if I come help you with the cleaning up?"

"And I'll come, too," Maisie eagerly added. "Auntie won't need me until supper time, so we'll get everything tidied in no time."

Jerusha's pride wanted to refuse the assistance, but she knew if she tried to do it alone, she'd fall behind in her other laundry. "If you want to help, I won't complain."

Singing began at the front of the room, so the ladies seated themselves quickly, Maisie with Mrs. Barry, Sheila with Lewis and their two small sons, and Jerusha in her usual place on the front row. To her amazement, Corporal Sutherland led the music with a pleasant, strong voice. After several hymns, he motioned for everyone to sit down.

"If y'all are like me, you feel a special sense of gratitude tonight, just being alive and unhurt, except for our preacher, here."

Jerusha didn't miss his possessive tone.

"Let's sing a verse of 'What Wondrous Love,' and then we'd like to hear your story of God's protection Sunday night."

Usually "testimony times" were slow at this little church. She'd often noticed how reluctant people seemed to be to share anything about themselves in public. She identified with the sentiment. But tonight, the singing halted for a full hour as one person after another told, some with shaking voices, how they had experienced Divine protection during the disaster. Even Lewis Murray spoke about being in town during the explosion and seeing men on either side of him thrown across the street by the blast, while he huddled safely against the side of a building. Mrs. Barry told about the large window in her kitchen being blown to bits without harming either her or her boarders. A young couple whom Jerusha hadn't seen before gave thanks the fire had been stopped just two houses away from where they lived. Ruth Pierce, the doctor's slender, dark-haired wife, thanked God for protecting her husband while he worked with the injured. David expressed his gratitude for the corporal being nearby when he'd been hit by flying debris.

Corporal Sutherland made his own contribution. "I'm sure many in our community are grateful for this church and for the generosity of the brother and sister who pastor us. In case you didn't know, the room where we're meeting tonight was an emergency aid station until this morning."

Jerusha wished her feelings came closer to those a "generous pastor" should feel. She felt no kinship with these people as they rejoiced. Stories of inexplicable happenings abounded, even outside the church. More than one man had staggered away from the heart of the disaster, while the person beside him had been killed. She'd heard more than twenty people had been killed. The parents and wives of the dead men probably weren't talking of God's protection. It had been a freak accident, making victims capriciously.

Thankfully, none of these pious people could read her mind. She wondered briefly if even God knew how she felt, then gave thanks He probably didn't care. She was doing her best to be the kind of person she should be. What would it matter to Him if her emotions didn't agree?

four

Jerusha pushed herself off her floor pallet shortly after 5:00 Thursday morning. She had slept uneasily, feeling like she'd been in a wrestling match all night. Though she still felt tired, sleep required more effort than getting up. She moved quietly around the piles of bedding still littering the cabin floor, trying not to disturb David. After discovering the freedom of crutches yesterday, who knew what he'd attempt today. She'd had a friend in Winnipeg who had been permanently crippled by improper healing of a broken bone. Jerusha feared for David's leg if he didn't take care of it. Being crippled wouldn't send him home, but it would make his work much more difficult. She tiptoed to the kitchen to check the stove. She'd need lots of hot water for the massive laundry project today. Having specific, direct action made it easier to get away from her thoughts.

"Mornin', Rushi."

Jerusha jumped, dropping the stove lid, and whirled around. "David! You're supposed to be sleeping."

Still in his pajamas, he grinned. "I slept enough yesterday for the next week. Besides, Keith and a couple of guys are coming over today to chop firewood and help clean up the meeting room."

"Who? What?" Jerusha wished she hadn't said anything the minute she heard her snappish tone.

"Hey, they're just coming to help. I know you're busy, so we'll stay out of your way."

She took a deep breath to steady herself. "I know, it's not a problem. I'm just tired."

"It's been a rough four days for you, eh? Keith's told me at least twice a day how much help you were in the aid station." He put a hand on her shoulder, and she heard a crutch clatter to the floor.

"Wouldn't be much of a pastor's daughter if I couldn't help people in trouble, now would I?" Bending down, she smiled tightly.

"You're more than a pastor's daughter, Rushi. You're my sister and a wonderful woman." Balanced once again, he leaned forward and kissed her cheek.

Jerusha hid her surprise behind a not entirely phony scandalized tone. "Reverend!"

"Whatsamatter, kid? I'm your brother, remember?" He grinned mischievously and clumped back to the bedroom. A series of bumps and grunts indicated he must be getting dressed. Jerusha sighed. Keeping him still would be harder than she thought. She probably ought to get dressed, too, before anything else happened.

She folded her nightclothes inside her floor pallet, which she folded in half and set in the corner behind a chair. The piles of bedding looked to be pretty well sorted, so the next step should be putting water on to heat. She might even get a couple of loads done before Maisie and Sheila arrived. Usually, she heated laundry water by setting the tubs directly on the stove and filling them there. However, David wouldn't be able to help her carry the tubs to the porch. She'd better use several large pots. It would be more cumbersome, but it remained the only solution available.

The bedroom had become silent. Had he returned to bed? Should she fix him breakfast or wait for him to appear again? Peeking in the doorway, she saw he was fully dressed and sitting on the bed with his legs stretched out in front of him and his back against the wall. His Bible lay open on his lap and he stared out the window. His lips moved slightly. An expression of almost tangible peace covered his face, varied only by his small smile and the happy crinkles around his eyes. *He is definitely demented*, Jerusha thought. What was there about this place, about his situation, to make him look so utterly contented, even happy? Yet she couldn't tear her gaze away from him. Maybe if she watched long enough, she'd figure out his secret.

He turned his head. "You're welcome to join me. I'm just telling our Father how glad I am He's brought us here, and also how grateful I feel that He sent you with me."

"David!" She wasn't sure whether she objected to his familiar way of talking about God, his joy at being in Dawson Creek, or his gratitude for her.

"Would you sit with me for a while? I'm sure the water won't scorch in your absence." His gentle teasing drew her to perch on the edge of the bed facing him. "You're distressed, aren't you, sister?"

She wondered what he'd think if he knew the complete truth. But if he knew, maybe he could help her discover how to find what he had. She settled for, "I'm concerned about you."

"And I'm concerned for you, so I guess that makes us a matched pair, eh?" His infectious chuckle stretched her mouth into an answering grin. "How am I worrying you?"

"What if your leg doesn't heal properly? Both the medic and the doctor said you have to keep still. If you don't, you could end up like Susannah Blake."

His forehead wrinkled in concentration. "Susannah—

oh, you mean the little girl from next door you used to play with?"

"She was crippled, David, because she broke her leg as a small child and it didn't heal properly."

"I remember her having a bit of a limp, but not crippled."

"She couldn't walk normally, and that's crippled in my book." Jerusha's voice sharpened involuntarily. "How would you like to be like that?"

"If that's the way things turn out, I'll learn to live with it. But it doesn't mean I have to stop living now."

"But pastors aren't supposed to be common laborers!"

"Hey, Rushi." His voice expressed gentle surprise. "We're in a frontier town. We all have to do things we're not used to, pastor included. That's part of building anything, be it a road, a church, or a town." When she didn't answer, he continued. "Don't waste energy resenting anything or anyone on my account, Sis. God called us, and He'll provide the help we need."

She couldn't swallow back the reply springing to her tongue. "He can't provide if people don't cooperate."

"They've got farms to tend, families to feed, and businesses to take care of. They give what they can. Just look at all the food they bring in for us."

"But vegetables, eggs, and milk alone won't finish the meeting room or give you decent clothes. They shouldn't have called you out here if they couldn't support you, or even help you build the church they say they want."

"Rushi, the church isn't the building. It's the people I'm learning to know and love, who provide support in ways money can't measure. Think of all the visitors we had last night, and the concern everyone expressed for people whose loved ones were killed this weekend. They could have just sat around being grateful it wasn't them. Besides, Keith and a couple of his men are coming to help today."

"So a bunch of army Yanks have to take care of us."

He spoke intently, but without rebuke. "If it weren't for an army Yank, I might not be here." He paused, then asked almost in a whisper, "Rushi, what's really making you unhappy? It's more than my leg and more than the church. Can you tell me?"

"I don't think God will do anything about it." She expected him to withdraw at her blasphemy.

Instead, he put a hand on her arm and asked tenderly, "Why not, kid?"

"Because I can't be the kind of person He expects me to be." The words came out defiantly.

"What do you mean?" Still no condemnation colored his tone.

"I hate being here! It's cold, dark, uncivilized, and lonely. Why couldn't God have called you somewhere safe and cultured? Why the edge of civilization in a dirty town overrun with heathen?"

"So you don't like Dawson Creek. That doesn't make you anything more or less than a human being with an opinion."

"But you actually enjoy it! What will people think of the church if they find out I hate this place?"

"Rushi, please look at me. You came because you felt you should, right?"

She nodded.

"Now that you're here, Dawson Creek is God's will for you, and Philippians promises He works in us to want to do His will."

"Then I must be doing something wrong."

"With our Heavenly Father, the issue isn't our doing, but our being. One of His delights is helping us learn to enjoy being the people He's made us to be."

"I don't think that's possible for me." She stood. "What do you want for breakfast?"

He looked at her for a moment, profound sadness in his blue eyes. Gradually, peace returned. "How about some of your marvelous coffee cake? We'll use the leftovers for snacking so we don't have to disturb you ladies."

Jerusha had already fed the second load of sheets through the wringer by the time Lewis, Sheila, and Maisie arrived. "They stopped by the house and offered me a ride. Who was I to refuse?" Maisie pulled her eyebrows up with mock innocence.

"Looks like you've been busy, and that's the truth," Sheila observed. "Shall I take these out to the clothesline?"

"Let me do that," Maisie interrupted quickly.

"Then I'll pump some more water for the stove."

This time Jerusha interrupted. "I just filled them."

Sheila's brown eyes twinkled with amusement. "All right, girls. 'Tis in the family way I am, not dying. I came to help. You have to let me do something."

Jerusha's gaze met Maisie's. Keeping Sheila from over-exerting herself would be difficult. "Let's pile the next load on this bench, and you can put them in the washtub without bending too much," Maisie suggested.

"Worse than Lewis, you are," Sheila declared with a saucy shake of her head.

The three worked companionably, Jerusha and Maisie making sure Sheila took only the lightest jobs. She often protested, but without resentment. Mid-morning she came up with her first idea the other two didn't override. "How about if I make some soup and cornbread for lunch? The menfolk will be hungry, and I don't think peeling carrots would be too much."

"If you sit down," Maisie and Jerusha chorused, then laughed at Sheila's disgusted appearance.

"Like a couple of mother hens, you two. But I thank ye. It's only for me best you're concerned."

"You're special," Maisie declared, "and so's your little one."

She and Jerusha managed to wash, wring, rinse, wring, and hang two more loads of blankets before the men trooped in from the meeting room ready for lunch. Jerusha was astounded to see half a dozen soldiers with the corporal as well as at least that many men from the church. They loudly praised the soup and cornbread, making Sheila's cheeks flame. Jerusha studied David's face carefully for signs of fatigue, but could only see how much he had enjoyed the activity.

"I'm making sure he doesn't overdo," a male voice whispered close to her as she set a stack of bowls in the dishpan.

She looked at Corporal Sutherland, who only winked and moved toward the door. "Let's get back at it, guys."

By midafternoon, the last of the bedding had been hung on the lines outside, and the first load had been brought in to thaw and finish drying. Conversation turned inevitably to the explosion.

"You should see the shop next to the warehouse," Sheila declared. "Nothing left but a pile of rubble."

"I noticed one of the hotels is pretty well flattened, too. The boardinghouse will be busier than ever, which means even more laundry for me." Jerusha sighed.

"I've heard the army is setting up temporary shelter. Did you know there are military patrols downtown every night?" Maisie's eyes sparkled.

"Whatever for?" Sheila didn't look nearly so thrilled.

"So many stores are missing walls, windows, or doors that the powers that be are afraid of looting. As soon as it gets dusk, the soldiers are out, and they don't leave until the sun's fully up."

"Which means from midafternoon to midmorning," Jerusha muttered to herself.

"And that's the truth." Sheila missed Jerusha's grumbling tone. "Makes me glad we're out on the farm."

"Where are the boys?" Maisie never missed an opportunity to hug and visit with the two youngsters.

"Lewis left them with a neighbor. He said I didn't need to be taking care of them and helping here, too."

"Not a bad idea." Maisie's eyes twinkled with new interest. "Is the baby to be a boy or a girl?"

"Lewis says it doesn't matter." Pain flitted across Sheila's face.

"And you?" Jerusha wondered.

A tear trickled down Sheila's cheek. "Only a boy."

Jerusha didn't know what to do. Undisguised emotion made her uncomfortable. But Maisie didn't hesitate. She moved quickly to Sheila's side and wrapped her arms around the woman. "What is it, Sheila?"

"You'll not tell anyone else, not even the reverend?" She looked at Jerusha.

"Of course not." Her answer came out more roughly than she intended, but Sheila seemed reassured.

She gulped a couple of breaths. "I'm so afraid this baby won't be a boy because I want one so much."

"Why a boy?" Maisie asked gently.

"I want Lewis to love me."

The quiet words hung in the air, almost drowned by chopping and hammering sounds beyond the walls. Jerusha opened her mouth to object, but Maisie's quick glance stopped her.

"Are you sure he doesn't already?"

Sheila shook her head forlornly. "How could he? I've done little but make mistakes since I came. I can sew cute outfits for his sons, but I can't cook a good meal. Now I'm in the family way, I can't even help him with the chores. Well, I could," she amended, "but he keeps asking me not to. If something happens to this baby, he'll never forgive me."

Her words baffled Jerusha. She'd assumed the boys were Sheila's as well. "You mean this is your first baby?"

Sheila's damp gaze regained a bit of humor. "Ye've not heard my story?"

Jerusha shook her head.

"Let's sit a spell while you tell it," Maisie suggested. She dished out squares of leftover coffee cake and poured coffee as if they were in her kitchen. Jerusha felt grateful for her sensibility and understanding.

"I grew up in Ireland, in case you couldn't tell," Sheila began with a chuckle, "the daughter of a dressmaker. Times were always rough, and Mum died when I was just thirteen. Too much work and not enough food. Dad had died when I was a baby. My older brothers found work in the factories, and I hired out as a dressmaker's apprentice. The lady who hired me treated me like a charity case. Anything I learned was by accident, as she felt I wasn't fit for anything but sweepin' floors. Then one day I saw a bit in the paper about farmers in Canada who were lookin' for wives. It said they'd pay our way if we'd just come. I slipped away in the night and made it to the shipping office. Lewis Murray met me at the station in Edmonton. His wife had died a couple of years before in birthin', and he wanted a mother for his little sons. Here I am, but it's not a very good wife I've been." Tears welled in her eyes again.

Though their situations were different, Jerusha felt Sheila's pain. She had those same feelings about her role. She squeezed the woman's hand. "I'm sorry."

Sheila smiled faintly. "At least he hasn't shipped me back."

"And he won't, I'm sure," Maisie declared firmly. "You mustn't worry so much, for the babe's sake. Have you prayed about it?"

Sheila's eyes glowed. "If it weren't for the Heavenly Father, I wouldn't have made it this far."

"Let's talk to Him again," Maisie suggested.

The two bowed their heads while Jerusha stared unseeingly past them. Both sounded so confident that Someone took a personal interest in their concerns. She felt on the outside of a precious secret, something she needed to know but couldn't find.

five

By the time Jerusha went to bed Friday evening, life felt almost back to normal, except for David still occupying her room. He tried to encourage her to sleep in the loft, but she didn't want to try the ladder. She'd become accustomed to sleeping on the floor even though real sleep remained elusive. As soon as she'd drift off, images would fill her mind—blood-stained people filling the meeting room, David lying limply in the corporal's arms, Winnipeg's culture and comfort, and most frequently, the peaceful expressions worn by David, Maisie, Sheila, and the corporal. She'd tried to be the right kind of person all her life. One of her few memories of her parents was kneeling by her mother's knee asking Jesus to forgive her for being a sinner and to help her be His kind of girl. She could still feel the trust in Him and love for Him she'd felt at that moment and in the months afterward. Eventually, though, an awareness of her responsibilities as a Christian replaced those childish emotions.

So she tossed her way through the night, waking only marginally refreshed. Two huge cloth bags of soiled bedding had been delivered the day before from the boardinghouse. She should be able to get the work done tonight so it could be delivered first thing Monday morning. The familiar frustration made her feel like screaming. Why should the pastor's sister have to work incessantly on public laundry? Granted, none of the church people seemed in the least offended, but that wasn't a mark in their favor. Church members with the proper respect for their pastor should be ashamed that his family would have to stoop to such work.

She lay in the early morning darkness, thinking of their pastor in Winnipeg. He had lived in one of the nicest homes in the city, and his wife's hands had never been as red and rough as Jerusha's. Mrs. Phillips had been one of the most refined ladies Jerusha knew, seeming to move through any situation with cultured detachment. How would she have handled the events of the past few days? Certainly Rev. Phillips never would have shown himself to his congregation with his leg swathed in boards and rags. Jerusha recalled the eagerness with which people had gathered around David. She couldn't remember seeing that kind of affection demonstrated for their minister. He, the Pastor, stood on a pedestal, separate from their everyday lives. It occurred to her that Mrs. Phillips probably didn't have the kind of friends Jerusha had found in Maisie and Sheila. In fact, Mrs. Phillips would probably have been horrified by their frank discussion of emotions and family life. Jerusha scrambled out of bed wondering if she'd ever find a resolution to her frustrations. Thank goodness there was still work to keep her occupied.

David slept longer this morning. Jerusha heard no movement from his room until close to 7:00. "Good morning, sleepyhead," she greeted him as he thumped toward the kitchen where she was scooting pots around to get laundry water heated.

He flashed a bright grin. "Good morning, yourself. I thought you said something yesterday about wanting me to rest more."

"So I did. You're learning."

He watched her carry several bucketfuls of water from the pump to the stove. "Guess that's easier in the washtub, isn't it?"

"Don't even think about it. This works just fine."

"Have I ever told you how much I appreciate your laundry work? I know it's not what you bargained for coming out here with me."

Jerusha laughed self-consciously. "I was wondering this morning what Mrs. Phillips would say if she saw me."

"I hope you don't feel you have to live up to her."

She didn't answer, concentrating instead on preparing oatmeal along with toast spread with David's favorite apple butter.

"How are your clotheslines holding up out there?"

"Just perfectly. They're a lot tighter in this cold than they were when you put them up, but not one has broken yet."

"I like that 'yet.'" He laughed. "Guess there's not much I can do to help, is there?"

"Just keep out of the way, and don't try to get too active."

By the time she had the washtubs filled, he had settled himself on the trunk bench along the wall, his leg propped in front of him and his Bible and notebook in his lap. "This okay, Mom?" he teased. "Figured I'd better have a sermon ready for tomorrow."

"At least you're sitting still for a change," she grumbled.

He only winked at her as he opened his books. Jerusha pushed the sheets down into the water with a specially made laundry plunger, forcing water through the fabric without getting her hands wet. After twenty minutes of washing, she used a long-handled wooden spoon to fish part of one of the sheets out of the water far enough to cool so she could touch it. Turning the handle of the wringer with one hand, she carefully fed the steaming sheet between the rollers, squeezing out soapy water. Mounted on a wooden frame between the two washtubs, the wringer fed the sheet into the hot rinse water. Only ten minutes of "plunging" were required for rinsing. She placed a board over the washtub, put her laundry basket on top of it, then directed the sheets back through the wringer into the basket. Three loads usually got the water so grimy, she had to empty the washtub, using a hose attached at one end to a hole in the bottom of the washtub. When not in use, the hose hooked over the edge of the tub. She drained the tub into a small metal pail, carrying each pailful outdoors and dumping it several feet away from the porch. A patch of icy brown snow showed where the wash water had been dumped on previous occasions. A few soap shavings and a bit of bleach turned the rinse water into fresh wash water, and she filled the empty tub with clean scalding water for rinsing. Periodically, David would say, "Listen to this, Rushi," and would read a portion of Scripture. His eyes always lit up like he'd made a wonderful discovery. Jerusha only heard long-familiar words that held little meaning.

Shortly after noon, the back door shuddered under strangely familiar blows. When she opened the door, Corporal Sutherland entered with a grin. "The Rev awake yet?"

She couldn't help smiling in reply. "Since seven o'clock, though he did sleep in a bit."

"Told you I'd take care of him." He removed his boots and stepped into the sitting room.

"Howdy, Preach! Thought your woodpile looked a little scrawny and figured I might be able to help."

"Much obliged. My sister's been rather hard on the supply with this laundry business of hers."

Jerusha was unprepared for the look of admiration on the soldier's face. "You do laundry as a business?"

She nodded.

"That's hard work! Who do you work for?"

"Mrs. Barry's boardinghouse. Any more than that and I don't think I'd have fingers left." She tried to laugh, wondering irrelevantly what her mother's hands looked like.

"Where do you dry all this stuff?"

As if to emphasize her point, she reached for her parka and winter boots.

"Outside. It freeze-dries."

"I thought your hands looked rather rough and sore the other night. No wonder, with hanging wet laundry in this cold."

"I've become used to it." She didn't mean to sound rude, but his concern made her uneasy. She hoisted the basket of wet blankets onto her hip, grabbed her bucket of clothespins, and hurried out the door. Just because she'd found tolerance for the job didn't mean she liked it. Before she'd finished hanging the blankets, she heard the rhythmic ring of the axe achieved only by an expert. Was there anything this man couldn't do well?

He chopped wood all afternoon, coming in periodically to warm up. David continued studying and reading portions of Scripture aloud, only getting up to make another pot of coffee for the corporal's next visit inside. Jerusha had just emptied the last tubful of wash water when he asked, "Mind if I invite Keith for supper?"

"I was only planning to have leftover stew and biscuits."

"Sounds great to me, but if you're bothered, I won't ask."

She could tell he really wanted the soldier to stay. "If you don't mind things being a little late, I could even throw together a dried apple cobbler."

"Thanks, Rushi." He looked straight at her with his special big-brother grin, the smile that said he knew her well and accepted her completely, the look that always made her wonder what he'd think if he knew how she really felt.

Settling dusk forced Corporal Sutherland to quit at the chopping block. He looked quickly at Jerusha before accepting David's invitation. "You've been pretty busy today. Sure you want to feed another hungry man?"

His consideration drew another smile from her. "Of course not. David needs the company."

The two chatted nonstop while she made biscuits. She heard David telling how he'd heard about Dawson Creek and decided to come. Over supper, he asked their guest how he'd arrived.

"Though I feel war is the greatest insult possible to human life, I knew I either had to join the army voluntarily or get drafted."

David reached for another biscuit. "Why not register as a conscientious objector?"

"It didn't seem like the direction I was supposed to take. I'd received a bit of emergency medical training, and checked into becoming part of the medical personnel. Next thing I knew, we were setting up camp here in Dawson Creek."

"Where did you grow up?" David's question echoed Jerusha's thoughts.

"On a farm in the northern part of the state of Colorado. The country's a lot like this area."

"Can't be as beautiful."

"You bet it is."

Both men spoke with conviction, and Jerusha wondered briefly if they'd lost their minds. She hadn't seen a single attractive aspect about this sprawling, half-built town, and goodness knew, she'd tried.

David had another question. "What are the people like there?"

"If you can believe it, a lot like people here, though more easily excited. I've found Canadians take a comparatively relaxed approach toward life. But in general, they're the same types, hardy farmers, dedicated to families, good neighbors, polite, not much tolerance for rowdy behavior."

"I know what you mean. I think Dawson Creek's still reeling from the arrival of the American hordes." David's grin took any sting out of his words.

"And I know as well as anyone what some of my countrymen can be like when they get a bit too much to drink."

"Anyone figure out yet what caused Sunday night's explosion?"

Corporal Sutherland studied his bowl for a few moments. "The army's not saying. The rumors I've heard indicate either someone was smoking too close to the hayloft at the livery stable or perhaps sabotage behind the area where Oman-Smith Company and Miller Construction had stored a bunch of dynamite which was supposed to be shipped out Monday. The livery went up in smoke before anyone realized what had happened, and by then it was too late to save the dynamite. Next thing we knew, BOOM!"

"Quite a few guys killed, I heard."

"That's even more hush-hush than the cause. Army's saying five civilians, but I don't see how that can be true.

There were just too many people hurt. There had to have been at least a dozen right in the building trying to stop the fire, not to mention the crew chain-handling the dynamite away from the storage area. I don't see how any of them could have made it when it blew. Of course, I'm not saying that as an army man."

"Just the stories we heard at prayer meeting the other night make you realize how close this whole town came to going up in bits. Do you have any idea how this is affecting army-civilian relations?" Typically, David appeared most concerned about keeping the peace.

"I guess town officials asked the army to set up martial law Sunday night, and the army's offered to bring in town planners to assist with reconstruction." A chuckle quivered in the corporal's voice.

Jerusha couldn't restrain an incredulous, "Town planners? Whatever on earth for?"

"It's not such a bad idea," David soothed. "I've heard the downtown block is pretty messed up, so what better time to rebuild it so it looks attractive, not to mention scientific in its organization."

She snickered. "It will take more than a couple of planners to bring scientific order to this place. I've never seen so much stuff piled on every square inch of unused ground—lumber, pipe, mechanical supplies, ammunition, not to mention jeeps, trucks, and tents."

Both men roared with laughter at her derision. "You'll have to excuse my sister," David gasped around his guffaws. "She's used to Winnipeg's well-ordered streets."

The corporal managed to bring his mirth under control. "I know the feeling, Miss Porter. Some days I feel like I'm just groping around in a vast outdoor warehouse, myself.

But maybe this will make you feel better. The army has also decided to give Dawson Creek a new water and sewer system."

"You mean running water, and drains that don't back up?" Jerusha thought of the unused pipe intended to carry waste water out of their house.

"Those in the know say the hordes which have moved to Dawson Creek or been stationed here have put such a load on the town's existing system as to make it unusable. Part of the army's compensation for Sunday night will be running water and working drains." He grinned at her expression.

"I'll believe it when I see it."

The conversation carried on while Jerusha cleared the table. The men set up a chess game in the sitting room, and she brought their dessert to them there. They discussed various people they knew who'd been directly affected by the fire or the explosion. Their caring for this town and the people in and around it sounded almost like a foreign language.

David invited Corporal Sutherland to stay for a devotional time, as well. They discussed several Scripture passages as though they'd made new discoveries that would make daily life more delightful. Jerusha listened half-heartedly, wishing she could share their enthusiasm. After a brief time of prayer, the corporal stood.

"This has been a most enjoyable evening, Reverend and Miss Porter. But I promised someone I'd help take good care of you, Rev, so I'm leaving before I keep you up too late." He grinned and David grimaced. He bundled into his coat and boots, then departed, leaving behind the same silence Jerusha had noticed Sunday night.

six

David finally disappeared into the bedroom for a nap on Monday afternoon just when Jerusha had begun to think he'd be up all day. He'd been on the go all day yesterday, preaching both in the morning and the afternoon, as well as visiting with the steady stream of guests who passed through their sitting room on Sundays. Jerusha had hoped he would need a nap today so she could slip out to deliver the clean laundry and pick up the next bag of soiled linen. David would object strongly if he knew, but she felt she had no choice. There was no way he could do the job for her.

She paused beside the bench outside Patterson's Men's Wear. Half a dozen blocks didn't seem that far until one had to lug an unwieldy bag the distance. She looked around at charred buildings and heaps of rubble. Others' reports hadn't been able to accurately convey the devastation. What she remembered of the area a week ago seemed civilized compared to the present destruction. It took a few moments to catch her breath, and she reached for the bundle again.

"Well, if it isn't the Reverend Porter's sister. And how is our minister feeling these days?"

Of all the people she could have met on this excursion, why did it have to be Sylvia Irvine, daughter of Dawson Creek's most prominent banker? Jerusha tried not to envy the young woman's woolen wrap trimmed in fur, her fashionable matching bonnet, or the mink muff expensively encasing her hands. "My brother's doing very well, thank you. He should be back on his feet in a couple of weeks."

"That must be a relief for you. I know I'd be just mortified having to carry laundry through town. I mean, it's bad enough if people guess what you're doing. But to be obliged to confirm their gossip! I guess spinsters learn to endure all kinds of disagreeable experiences." She tittered shrilly.

Jerusha ignored the inner voice that verified Sylvia's comments and squelched the urge to slap her. "I imagine we've all had to do disagreeable things since last Sunday."

A spark of anger replaced condescension in the young woman's blue-eyed gaze, but her voice remained silky. "That must have been just terrible for you, your brother being hurt like that and then having our beautiful little church invaded by American soldiers. However did you endure it?" Her expression implied only a woman of inferior sensibilities could have refrained from hysterics.

Jerusha mentally reached for her friendliest smile. "It's amazing what one can do when people need help."

Sylvia glanced over Jerusha's shoulder, her expression barely betraying surprise. She tittered again, this time nodding regally. "I look forward to seeing you and your dear brother this Sunday."

Jerusha reached for the laundry bag, only to feel it slip from her grasp. She whirled to face Corporal Sutherland. "It's you! I wondered what frightened her away."

"Frighten? No." He solemnly shook his head, his lips pressed into a thin line, though his eyes looked friendly enough. "She'd just been so busy taunting you she didn't realize I was standing behind you the whole time."

She felt ready to sink through the boardwalk or hide in

the nearest snowbank. Sylvia's attitude had been humiliating enough without this man being a witness. "May I have my bag, please?"

"No." This time his lips smiled, too. "I agree with Miss Irvine that you shouldn't be carrying this, but only because it's far too heavy. I think your willingness to work hard right along with your brother is admirable. I can guess where you're going. Have you heard Dawson Creek's downtown is going to be built with brick and stucco buildings?"

"Won't they look kind of out of place with the buildings we still have?" The trivial talk restored Jerusha's sense of balance, though she wondered why she felt so comfortable visiting with him.

"I think the present buildings are either going to be replaced or get new false fronts." He glanced around them. "Isn't winter a gorgeous time of year? The way it snows around here reminds me so much of home. But I do miss being on the farm and looking out over fields covered in soft, undisturbed white. Towns and army camps make winter look dingy and depressing."

Dingy and depressing. Those were just the words Jerusha would have chosen to describe winter, at least in Dawson Creek. In Winnipeg—she stopped herself. She simply had to quit comparing the two places.

The corporal interrupted her mental treadmill. "Have you ever been cross country skiing, Miss Porter?"

"The only winter sport I've tried is skating. The skating parties back home used to be the big youth social events of the winter."

"I've heard there are some wonderful trails around here where it would be easy to learn to ski. How do you think

David would feel about a youth ski trip?"

She had the uncomfortable feeling David would think it a terrific idea. Why she didn't agree, she couldn't say. She only wished heartily this man wouldn't be so...she searched for the right word...so *interested* in them. "I'm not sure what David would think, since neither of us have skis."

"That could be rectified easily enough." He grinned at her as though he realized her objections had nothing to do with equipment.

With relief she saw the boardinghouse across the street. "Thanks for helping me with this bag. I'm sure David will thank you, too."

"Is there another bag to be picked up?"

She'd been wondering how she would get the bag of soiled linen home, since crumpled sheets filled a bigger bag than folded ones. Though she wanted strongly to cut this encounter short, she knew she couldn't carry the laundry alone. "Yes."

"May I help?"

The twinkle in his gray eyes made her feel like he wanted her to try to refuse. She lifted her chin a notch. "I'd be obliged, Corporal."

"My friends call me Keith," he growled, then kept up a steady flow of conversation until they reached the parsonage. Though his words and tone stayed light and cheerful, Jerusha felt there was more to this man than she could see, something that both attracted her and made her feel uneasy.

David had awakened and sat waiting in the sitting room when she returned. She'd barely opened the door when his don't-interrupt-me tone greeted her. "Jerusha, I know where you've been and you knew I wouldn't approve. We don't need both of us injured. Besides, downtown can be a rough place for a woman alone these days, especially with all the army personnel hanging around. You know I'm not all strung out on appearances, but sometimes a little discretion is advisable."

Corporal Sutherland had touched her shoulder briefly as soon as the tirade began. His wink silenced her defense. He remained out of sight until David's words ran out. A long pause ensued until David asked, less sure of himself, "Jerusha?"

The corporal stepped through the doorway between the porch and sitting room. "She's been with me, Rev."

If Jerusha had been an artist, she would have immediately reached for pencil and paper to capture David's expression. Frustration, relief, and embarrassment vied for dominance until humor won out. "Well, I guess that serves me right for getting so uptight. I shouldn't have jumped to conclusions."

"Oh, you weren't entirely wrong," the corporal assured him with a reproving glance at Jerusha. "I just managed to interrupt her stubbornness before it got her in trouble."

"How far did she get?"

Being discussed like a small child only added to Jerusha's discomfort with her rescuer and her lingering humiliation at Sylvia's hands. "I made it just fine to Patterson's. While I appreciate the corporal's assistance, I don't see I had any other choice. I've been hearing ever since I came about how people on the frontier do what they have to do. Well, I did it. If it upsets you so much, you can ship me home where I belong." To her further mortification, a sob escaped on the last word, and she fled to her room without thinking. The sound of the door slamming behind her brought small relief. She lay face down on the bed, feeling her tears wet the pillow. Though she felt embarrassed by her emotionalism, somehow weeping brought release. Her pride wanted her to get up and face the men immediately as though nothing were wrong, but profound weariness kept her in place.

Eventually, a quiet tap on her door roused her. When she didn't reply, she heard crutches thump near her bed and felt David sit beside her. His hand gently massaged the back of her neck. "I'm sorry, Rushi. I overreacted. Keith told me about Sylvia Irvine. I wish I could have spared you that. I know Dawson Creek is nothing like what you're used to, and I'm sorry I haven't told you more often how much I appreciate your being here with me. I know it's not easy, but you handle it well. I love you, Sis. I wish I could help you accept yourself just as you are. You don't have to live up to anything or be anything other than yourself."

His quiet murmuring managed to reach the always painful place inside her that had become so inflamed since the explosion. She felt unworthy of his words, yet they were a healing balm she couldn't refuse. She turned to look at him with a watery smile. "Thanks."

He extended a paper-wrapped package to her. "Keith asked me to give this to you."

Puzzlement wrinkled her forehead. Why would he be leaving a gift for her?

"Go ahead and open it. I'm sure it's not dynamite."

She sat up and cautiously pulled the paper away. Two bright yellow pieces of fruit lay within the folds. "Lemons?"

"Yeah. He said if you use a thin slice to smear the juice

on your hands after laundry, it will help keep your skin from getting so dry and sore."

She wanted to take offense at the corporal's notice of her most embarrassing feature, but something whispered that he hadn't meant to offend. In fact, it appeared he might even care about her as a person, not just as David's sister. "Lemon juice seems like a strange skin tonic."

"Maybe next time he stops by, he'll tell you why it works."

"Maybe so." She stared at the fruit, not sure what to do with the feeling of being the object of concern.

"Rushi?" David's quiet tone made her look into his face. "I think Keith Sutherland wants to be your friend as well as mine. Will you please let him do so, for my sake?"

She didn't feel comfortable with the suggestion. "Why for your sake?"

"Because I'd like you to have someone you can trust besides me."

"You're not planning to hurt yourself again, are you?" Only with her brother did she feel comfortable enough to tease.

Though his eyes twinkled, his face remained serious. "I'd just feel more comfortable knowing there was someone else you could turn to if you needed help."

She thought she understood what had prompted his request. "I'm sorry I worried you this afternoon."

He smiled. "I shouldn't have let myself get so upset, just like I'm not going to let you evade the question. You'll let him be your friend, Rushi?"

Though she couldn't bring herself to look directly at him, she nodded. How else could she respond to his uncharacteristic plea?

seven

The following Saturday, Jerusha found herself among a group of excited young adults in horse-drawn wagons headed for some snow-covered fields beyond the town. David had eagerly endorsed the corporal's idea of a skiing excursion, and word had spread quickly. Some of the young adults from the church had invited friends, and several of the single men from Mrs. Barry's boardinghouse joined the party. Corporal Sutherland was accompanied by a dozen soldiers. Sylvia Irvine quickly made conquests of at least half of the young men. Jerusha planned to spend the afternoon sitting by the campfire with David.

The wagons turned down a rough road between some low-growing trees. Before Sylvia had a chance to complain, they creaked to a stop. In an unbelievably short amount of time, the young men had a bonfire crackling and several makeshift benches set up around it. Jerusha watched her companions quickly strap on their skis and slide away. Corporal Sutherland made sure David had a place to elevate his leg and plenty of blankets. Jerusha turned to find Maisie, but she'd already been whisked away by an eager soldier.

"Ready for your first skiing lesson, Miss Porter?" the corporal teased.

"I told you I have no skis." She tried to smile away the harshness of her words.

"Never underestimate an American soldier." He grinned

and slapped a pair of skis onto the snow in front of her. "I even found a pair of ski boots which I think might be your size."

Jerusha only gaped at him, not believing the circumstances which had put her in this embarrassing position.

"Don't wait around on my account, Rushi," David offered from nearby. "Once you get the hang of it, you'll have a great time."

She glared at her brother, who only smiled back encouragingly. His wink reminded her of their conversation concerning this unsettling man.

"Boots off." The corporal's voice discouraged argument.

Reluctantly, Jerusha unlaced her boots, suddenly grateful David had bullied her into wearing a pair of his pants, ridiculous though she felt. She'd insisted a pastor's sister had no business wearing men's clothes, and he'd insisted no sensible human being would venture out for an afternoon in the snow with only a long woollen skirt for warmth. No sooner had she removed one boot than the corporal replaced it with a ski boot. Before she had time to protest further, he'd slipped skis under her feet and snapped them into place.

"Let's go." He grasped both her gloved hands to pull her to a standing position. The skis started to slip out from under her, but he firmly held her upright. "Don't tense up. Just stand for a couple of minutes and you'll get used to the feeling. Keep your knees loose."

Jerusha had no idea what he meant, but found she had no time to contemplate it. She wanted to dispose of his arms around her as quickly as possible. That meant learning to stand on these slippery boards. It turned out to be only a little more difficult than standing on ice skates.

He released her long enough to hand her a set of poles, then reached for his own. "Don't try to fight the way the skis slide. Try to move with it. Like this." He skied a little ways from her, then back. "You'll balance best if you move your right arm with your left foot and vice versa. Sounds weird, but you'll get the rhythm."

Gradually, they worked their way toward the trees and away from the fire. Jerusha could hear laughter from the crowd ahead and wondered what they thought of her alone with the corporal. As her concentration wavered, so did her coordination. The skis started to slide faster than she could keep up.

"Whoa, there." The corporal quickly steadied her so she could pull her feet back under her control. "Shouldn't try to worry and ski at the same time," he advised with a grin. "Skiing was meant for relaxation."

"Then why don't you go relax?"

If he wondered at her sharp tone, his face didn't show it. He only grinned again. "Because this is more fun."

She laughed sarcastically. "You can't be serious. Why would you want to spend the afternoon teaching me to ski?"

He looked at her intently for a moment, then replied quietly, "Because I'd like to get to know you."

Jerusha didn't know how to answer. *If he does, he'll wish he hadn't.* Yet, she'd promised David. Her companion didn't try any more conversation until they had rounded a group of trees and were working their way back toward the campfire. She let her gaze drift toward Sylvia, who'd removed her skis and now hovered around David, rearranging his blankets.

"You agreed with what she said to you on Monday, didn't you?" He asked the question gently, omitting any hint of criticism.

Jerusha's gaze snapped to his face, where compassion hovered in his eyes. "How did you know?"

"I didn't. I just guessed. But I'd like to know why you left Winnipeg."

"David was called here to pastor the church."

"Were you called, too?"

"Of course. I'm his sister." Her tone sharpened at the gentle probing near her most painful emotions.

His forehead wrinkled momentarily, then he continued skiing slowly enough that she could keep up. "Any family back home?"

"Just Uncle Cam and Aunt Vivienne. She's frightened David's going to get married and I'll be stranded out here." She chuckled, relieved he'd moved his inquiries to safer ground.

"She's a worrier?"

"Not really, but propriety is very important to her."

"What were your pastor and his wife like?"

She pondered for a moment. "Well-educated, also concerned about appearances, refined, almost aristocratic. I admire them both."

"I can tell." He smiled encouragingly. "What did he teach about God?"

"I can't remember him ever talking much about God, except at revival time. Most of his sermons were about maintaining Christian testimony or how wonderful the Bible characters were. God always seemed kind of remote." She almost gasped at her statement, hardly believing that she, a minister's offspring, had dared say such a thing. "I didn't mean—"

He smiled again, this time reassuringly. "I think I know

what you meant. Don't worry, I don't think anyone else heard you." He winked. "Just between us, what do you think of God?"

Jerusha felt alarm prickle all over her. "What do you mean?"

"Some people see God as a benevolent grandfather type, always wanting to make us feel good. Others view Him as a dictator, waiting to strike us down if we do something wrong. To my way of thinking, He's a loving Father, Who carefully manages the details of my life so as to bring me the most joy."

Jerusha felt almost dizzy. The God he described bore no resemblance to the One she tried so hard to serve. Was this man crazy or incredibly wise? He was watching her expectantly, waiting for her reply. "I don't...uh, I mean..."

"Hot chocolate's on!" Maisie's call from the bonfire interrupted the conversation.

"Let's go get it before they drink it all." The corporal seemed not to notice she hadn't answered his question.

Jerusha's fear of falling hampered her impulse to hurry. She never should have allowed this conversation to take place. She should have been where Maisie stood now, handing out steaming cups, making sure everyone was comfortable, keeping an eye on David. As soon as the corporal showed her how to release her boots from the skis, she hurried to her friend's side. "What can I do to help?"

Maisie smiled brightly. "Absolutely nothing. This is your afternoon to relax and enjoy yourself."

Jerusha smiled weakly, wishing she hadn't let herself be pushed into this. Maybe she should have just stayed home. Fortunately there was an empty place on the bench beside David.

"What's skiing like, Sis?"

The corporal's questions had completely distracted her, but she couldn't tell David that. "It's not skating, but it'll do."

He hugged her shoulders. "I hope you're having a good time."

A shrill titter warned of Sylvia's approach. "How nice to see you out here with us, Miss Porter! You've been working so hard lately, I haven't been able to visit with you nearly as often as I'd like." She giggled and fluttered around in front of David.

Jerusha looked at David appealingly, but his expression indicated he noticed nothing amiss. He actually smiled at Sylvia. "How are you enjoying skiing, Miss Irvine?"

"I've never been as robust as your sister, so I find too much exercise quite fatiguing. However, the company is extremely pleasant. You must be bored to tears here all by yourself."

Jerusha looked around for Maisie, needing desperately to get away from Sylvia. The girl's affected manners aroused both Jerusha's envy and disgust. The veiled insults pushed her perilously close to tears. Maisie still stood by the bonfire, surrounded by laughing people, refilling cups. Jerusha looked around the group of young people wondering why she felt so uncomfortable while everyone else was obviously having fun. A pair of gray eyes on the other side of the bonfire stopped her gaze. A bold wink preceded a smile, then the corporal stood and walked toward her.

"How about another lesson? I promise I won't ask any questions this time."

If she didn't know better, Jerusha would have thought he

knew how she felt and was trying to cheer her up. She pushed the tempting thought away, accepting his offer as simple courtesy. "Thank you, Corporal."

Rather than releasing her hand when she stood, he tucked it into the crook of his elbow. She tried to pull away but he held on firmly. "I'm not letting you go until you promise to call me Keith, as do the rest of my friends. Only army folk call me Corporal, and I've never liked the sound of Mr. Sutherland." His eyes twinkled down at her.

"I can't do that!"

"Why not?" He appeared to enjoy her discomfort.

"It's not proper. Now please let me go."

"Life's not nearly so formal out here. No one will even notice, I'm sure."

She couldn't tell whether he meant his holding her hand or the form of address he'd requested. Either way, her answer remained applicable. "It's inappropriately familiar."

He released her hand when they reached the bench where he'd left their skis and poles. "If I thought you were truly as offended as you sound, I'd apologize. Instead, I'm going to propose a contest. If I get my skis on and am standing first, you call me Keith. If you win, you may call me anything you like."

His ridiculous proposal startled her into laughter, something she hadn't felt like doing in months. The challenge in his eyes made her banish thoughts of propriety. But she wouldn't win if she didn't take control of the situation quickly. "It's a deal. Go!" She gave the command and reached for her skis at the same time. The right boot didn't want to fit easily into the binding, but she jammed it in place. She grabbed her poles, but found the other ends of them trapped in the snow by a large boot.

The corporal sat watching her, his shoulders vibrating with silent laughter. "I didn't think you had it in you."

Jerusha couldn't stop the grin that pulled at her lips. His enjoyment was too infectious. "You haven't even started."

His grin faded. "I didn't think you'd take me so seriously. Besides, I want you to consider me your friend because that's what you want, not because I've insisted."

"Thank you, Corporal." She hated to see the disappointment in his eyes. But she didn't feel ready to consider him a friend, despite her promise to her brother. He'd already come too close to perceiving the person she still tried to hide from herself.

She expected him to ski away and join the others. Instead, he put his skis on and slowly led to the area where she'd been practicing earlier. For the rest of the afternoon, he stayed close to her, though not close enough to make her uncomfortable. When it came time to return to town, he was on hand to help her into the wagon. She couldn't be positive, but it seemed he made sure she and David were the last two in their wagon group to be dropped off.

"Hope you didn't get too chilled today, Rev," he said as he stopped the horses beside the parsonage.

"Not a chance." David's voice held a gentle smile. "I was well taken care of."

Jerusha immediately pictured Sylvia hovering, rearranging blankets, making small talk. David couldn't possibly think her pleasant company!

"I enjoyed the day, too, thanks to your sister," Corporal Sutherland commented. "She's getting quite handy on those skis."

"I could never beat her on skates, so it doesn't surprise me." David laughed, leaning on the corporal until Jerusha handed him his crutches. "Would you like to come in for a snack?"

The corporal looked at Jerusha for a moment before replying. "Thanks for the offer, but I have a couple of things I need to take care of back at camp."

David nodded and clumped into the house. Jerusha didn't follow him immediately, though she couldn't have explained why. She looked uncertainly at Corporal Sutherland.

His gaze met hers. "How are the hands?"

"They stung pretty badly the first couple of times I tried it, but the juice seems to be helping." She felt glad her gloves covered the subject of discussion.

"I figured it might hurt to start with, since your hands got so cracked. It's actually the soap residue left on your hands that dries them so badly. The lemon juice cuts through the soap. They should be healed up in no time."

She didn't feel in a hurry to end the conversation, despite the cold. "Where did you find lemons in this town?"

"Never underestimate the army." He grinned briefly. "I really did enjoy spending time with you today."

"I had fun, too."

His eyebrows twitched with amusement. "You don't get as much fun as I think you need. I'd like to fix that if I may."

"Building a church takes a lot of work." She smiled to show she didn't mean to be ungracious.

"But God's the One Who invented laughter." He studied her silently again. "I'll be back, and in the meantime, I'll be praying you meet His love."

He jumped up into the wagon and guided the horses down the street. She watched his departure, feeling again the prickly alarm from his questioning, accompanied by a strange sense of anticipation.

eight

David's leg mended quickly. A little over a month after the explosion, he walked with only a slight limp. The town recovered more slowly. Most store fronts had been restored, though the livery barn remained a burned-out pile of rubble. The army's official word still held the casualty count at only eight soldier and no civilians, but rumors placed the total anywhere between two dozen and two hundred soldiers and civilians. The army's reluctance to discuss the matter increased Dawson Creek residents' continuing distrust.

"It's just not right," eighteen-year-old Greg McEvan declared one evening when a number of young people gathered at the parsonage for an informal social. His red hair lay in disarray from his vigorous head shaking, and his gray eyes flashed with indignation. "If the army hadn't been here, the explosion never would have happened in the first place."

"I heard it happened because of a fire in the livery barn. That could have happened regardless," David suggested quietly.

"But the explosion caused the damage, and it happened only because the army insisted on storing the dynamite here in town instead of at Mile Eight where they're supposed to."

Maisie refilled Greg's coffee cup. "Mr. Skillings at the telegraph office said the drivers needed a special permit to haul it out of town and had to wait overnight."

"Like I say, those Americans have to make everything so complicated. What's wrong with taking the stuff straight to Mile Eight?"

"There's nothing we can do about it now, son," Mrs. Barry soothed. She had accompanied Maisie as she often did and was welcomed by the young people like a beloved grandmother. She turned to Jerusha. "This cake is delicious! How do you find time for baking with all the laundry we've had to send you? I've worried about working you too hard."

Jerusha wondered briefly why she found Mrs. Barry's questions unoffensive and Sylvia's painful. "I appreciate the business, and with David back on his feet, we're managing."

Dr. and Mrs. Pierce had also stopped by for a quick visit. Dr. Pierce cleared his throat. "I wish for both of your sakes we could afford to pay our pastor a full salary. It would be nice if you didn't have to 'manage,' as you put it, Miss Porter."

She couldn't ignore the genuine affection on their faces. It seemed incomprehensible that these people should actually love her. Ministers' families traditionally received respect, but love? "I've noticed everyone out here works hard. I don't think the minister's sister should be an exception." She tried to smile graciously while she carried away empty plates and cups. All of life since the explosion seemed designed to make her uncomfortable, unsure of herself and her role. As if the conversation had taken place earlier in the day, she unwillingly recalled Corporal Sutherland's words during the skiing party. "I see God as a loving Father, controlling the details of my life to bring the most joy to me." She bid the Pierces goodbye, expressing hopes they would stop again soon, served more tea and coffee, and started dishes, all the while embroiled in her own thoughts. *Joy.* Not a dominant element in her life, she realized. But then love wasn't a concept she readily associated with God, either. Duty, responsibility, sacrifice, good works, proper behavior—those were the qualities found in good Christians. She could almost picture God with a checklist, evaluating her and finding her lacking.

Maybe that explained why Corporal Sutherland hadn't been around since the skiing party. She'd tried not to notice his absence from church, as well as from their sitting room. Had he evaluated her and also found her wanting? She recalled her reluctance to answer his question about God. What did she think about God, anyway, and why did wondering make her so uncomfortable?

"May I help with the dishes?" Maisie's voice startled her.

"Only if you want to." Jerusha studied her friend's face. "I can handle it if you'd rather visit."

"Of course I'd like to help you. How about if I wash? Then you can put things away in their proper places instead of hunting for them until next week."

Jerusha couldn't think of any light conversation. Maisie didn't seem to mind the silence, though she looked quizzically at Jerusha from time to time. Before she realized what she was doing, Jerusha spoke her thoughts. "Maisie, what do you think of God?"

Maisie looked momentarily startled, then her face softened and a smile lit her eyes from deep inside. "I'd say He's my Friend. Sometimes He's like a loving Father to me, but mostly a Friend who knows me better than I know myself. Why do you ask?"

Jerusha didn't know how to explain herself. What would Maisie think if she knew her doubts? "I don't know. People out here seem to think of Him differently than the people back ho—in Winnipeg." She hoped Maisie hadn't noticed her slip.

"Can you give me details?" Maisie looked genuinely interested. Though Jerusha examined her face closely for condemnation, she found nothing but friendly concern.

"Like the day you and Sheila helped me clean up after the explosion. You prayed for her baby, and it seemed like you really believed God cared. Sheila said that day she didn't think she would have survived what's happened to her if it hadn't been for God. Back home, no one talks much about Him. Prayers are for church. I've never heard anyone pray before about personal things. After the explosion, people talked like God really did protect them."

"You don't think He did?" Again, Maisie's face held no criticism.

Jerusha looked straight into her eyes. "This may be shocking, but I don't know. My mother told me about Jesus dying on the cross when I was little. I remember asking Him to be part of my life at that time, and for awhile, I felt like I knew Him. But my awareness of Him faded with childhood. Now, He just seems distant and hard to please."

"Have you talked to your brother about it?"

Jerusha studied the dish towel in her hands. "No. What kind of a minister's sister am I if I don't even know who God is?"

"An honest one. I don't know nearly as much about the Bible as the reverend, but I don't think God minds if we ask questions. I know my dad never got upset with me for asking questions, and I'm sure God has more patience than my dad." Maisie dried her hands and wrapped her arms around Jerusha. "Whatever the case, Jerusha, I only think of you as my friend. You could tell me you didn't believe in God at all and I'd still love you."

Tears filled Jerusha's eyes. She awkwardly returned Maisie's hug, wondering what to do with the strange emotions she felt. Did Maisie really mean what she'd said? Though the sentimental moment passed, and they joined Mrs. Barry and David for a game of dominoes, Jerusha's mind continued to contemplate possibilities.

After losing the third game, David stretched and yawned. "I'm not sure I can handle getting beaten again. You ladies play a tough game."

Mrs. Barry smiled at Jerusha. "We really should be going. We have a long day tomorrow, since Saturday's our cleaning day. Thanks for a lovely evening."

David reached for his Bible. "Would you stay long enough to join us in evening devotions?"

Mrs. Barry nodded. "We'd be honored."

David raised his voice to talk above the noise of the dozen or so young adults still visiting and playing checkers. "Mrs. Barry needs to leave soon, but I've asked her to stay for our devotional." He handed his Bible to her. "I'd like to hear you read my favorite passage, if you would, Mrs. Barry. Romans chapter five, verses one through eleven." The room quieted almost instantly as people found places to sit and turned to face David.

Jerusha had often heard a strange love in David's voice when he read Scripture. Tonight, she heard the same affectionate anticipation in Mrs. Barry's reading. Then the words themselves captured her attention. "'But God commendeth

His love toward us..." Mrs. Barry read on, but the phrase replayed itself in Jerusha's mind. Though it had been years since Scripture reading had meant anything more than religious words, tonight the single sentence felt like a refreshing drink to her thirsty soul. She waited impatiently for David to finish praying and for the guests to leave so she could ask David about her discovery.

Well over an hour later, he closed the door behind the last group. "What is it, Rushi? Your eyes have lit up like candles."

She laughed self-consciously. "I heard something tonight, and it sounds almost too good to be true." Suddenly she felt tongue-tied. How could she explain her thoughts to her minister brother? "I've been wondering about God." She waited for his shocked exclamation.

"Have you reached any conclusion?" He lowered himself onto the bench, his gaze remaining lovingly on her face.

She had to ask a question of her own before she could answer his. "Aren't you ashamed of me for even wondering?"

His face softened with a gentle smile. "No. Actually, I've been praying you would start asking questions."

"Why?"

He patted the seat beside him. "Come sit and I'll try to tell you."

"Do you want coffee or more cake?"

"Not now, Rushi." He patted the seat again. "I just want you to relax with me for awhile." When she seated herself, he put his arm around her shoulders and leaned against the wall. "It started a long time ago, soon after you became a teenager. I've watched your gentle love for Jesus be replaced by a compulsion to live up to what you think you should be, what you think our mother is."

She gasped at his accuracy, never having faced her own feelings so bluntly. "What's wrong with wanting to be like Mom? Aunt Vivienne has told us often what a wonderful woman she is."

"But you've forgotten Mom is human. I remember how much she loves God, but also how much she loves life. I remember her laughing with us kids, helping us play jokes on Dad. She isn't perfect, Rushi. I also have memories of her getting flaming mad at Dad, impatient with people in the church who didn't share her enthusiasm for missions. Then time would calm her down, she'd ask forgiveness of people she'd spoken unkindly to, and she'd spend time talking the matter over with God and accepting His forgiveness. Somewhere you've been handed the idea you have to be something Mom never was, and in the process you've lost the awareness of God's love Mom tried so hard to teach us."

The Scripture passage played through her mind again while she considered her response. Part of her felt betrayed by his recollections while another part wanted to hear more of what he remembered. *"But God commendeth His love toward us..."* Could it really mean what it sounded like? She decided to be blunt. "That's what I've been wondering about. Corporal Sutherland said something while we were skiing about how he thinks of God as a loving Father. Maisie said she sees Him as her Friend. You obviously think of Him as a Friend, too. Somehow I just can't share your perspective."

"How do you see Him, Rushi?"

She thought for several minutes, still not sure she wanted

to reveal exactly how unpastoral her thinking had become. But then again, what did she have to lose? He couldn't very well kick her out of the house. But would he still love her? "I don't know. I guess kind of like some sort of faraway person Who keeps track of how well I'm living up to what He expects."

"And what do you think He expects?" David's voice had lost none of its gentle affection.

"To be the right kind of pastor's sister and daughter. I guess like Mrs. Phillips. Always saying the right thing, always looking my best, never upset by anything, always eager to help the people in our church..." Her voice trailed off as she realized the enormity of her expectations.

"What about what Jesus said about the whole law being wrapped up in two commandments, to love God and to love our neighbor as ourselves?"

"I don't measure up there, either. Some days I don't even like the people around here, much less love them. And God seems too remote for me to love." She turned so she could see his reaction.

His gentle eyes met her gaze. "Have you thought about how much He loves you?"

"I've wondered how He can when I'm so far from the kind of person He wants me to be. But one of the verses Mrs. Barry read tonight said He loved us when we were sinners, or did I hear it wrong?"

A gleam of joy lit his eyes. "That's the point exactly, Rushi. His love for us has nothing to do with what we do or how we behave. He just loves us."

She shook her head, unable to reconcile David's words with her mental image of a Supreme Being with a checklist. "It sounds too good to be true."

"God solves that problem, too." David grinned. "According to Him, it doesn't matter what we believe or don't believe. He tells us how it is in Scripture, and that's the way it is. Most of our difficulties come from our efforts to reconcile our own ideas with what He says about Himself, rather than simply accepting—"

A loud pounding at the back door stopped him. He hurried to respond. "Lewis Murray! What can we—"

Mr. Murray's panic-stricken voice interrupted. "Hello, Reverend. I need your sister. My wife's in labor and she's calling for Miss Porter."

Overhearing the conversation, Jerusha gasped and ran for her coat. Concern for her friend thrust her questions out of her mind. Without a miracle, Sheila's baby would be born far too early to survive.

nine

Jerusha could think of nothing to say as Lewis threw her small overnight bag into the back of his old truck, then assisted her into the cab. What if Sheila lost her baby! The thirty-minute ride to the Murray farm seemed interminable.

The truck had barely stopped when both Lewis and Jerusha threw the doors open and ran for the small, two-storey log farmhouse. Even from the porch she could hear Sheila's cries of pain.

"I left my boys with the neighbor." Lewis seemed to be trying to explain something. "They love her so much." He turned abruptly, striding off the porch into cold darkness.

Jerusha pushed the front door open, uncertain of where to find her friend. The next cry seemed to come from the back bedroom. She tiptoed to where Sheila lay in the middle of the big bed, which showed evidence of her intense thrashing. Tears ran from her closed eyes down her cheeks. Jerusha had never seen a birthing before. She felt as helpless to provide emotional support as medical assistance. Why had Sheila asked for her, rather than Maisie? Another spasm gripped Sheila, and this time she screamed. Jerusha lost her uncertainty in desperation.

She smoothed the wet, tangled hair away from her friend's face, then reached for the young woman's hand. "I'm here, Sheila, just like you asked."

"Jerusha?" Sheila looked around the room.

"Right here. What can I do for you?"

"Make it stop." The tears poured down her face again. "I'm going to lose the baby, and he's never going to forgive me."

Jerusha didn't know where the words came from. She just started talking. "It's not your fault, Sheila. Sometimes babies just come too early. Lewis cares for you, and he still will after this is over."

"But I wanted to give him another son, and now I'm losing it." Hysteria edged her voice.

"Sheila, please calm down. For now, don't think about Lewis. Concentrate on keeping as relaxed as you can."

"But it hurts. And my baby's going to die!" Another spasm squelched her sobs. She grabbed Jerusha's hand so hard it hurt. Her back arched with pain, emphasizing her gently rounded abdomen. Another moan came through her clenched teeth.

"Can I help?" The ragged whisper came from the doorway where Lewis' white face looked as agonized as his wife's. Sheila heard the whisper and began sobbing again.

Jerusha had a feeling his presence would only make his wife worse. She gently steered Lewis away from the bedroom. "Have you called Doctor Pierce?"

"Yeah. He's at Anderson's. Louise is having her baby. Ours wasn't supposed to come yet!" The normally quiet farmer slammed his fist onto the nearby kitchen table.

"Only God can stop a baby once it decides to come." Jerusha felt like an idiot, but what else could she say?

But the words seemed to calm the tall man. "I'd forgotten He cares, too." He leaned against the wall with his head bowed for a few moments. Then he looked Jerusha in the eyes. "Please tell me what to do."

She didn't know how to say it. "Sheila's pretty upset.

Um...well, maybe if you didn't...I mean..."

He was already nodding. "I'll try to stay away from the room. Can I bring anything for you?"

His understanding overwhelmed her. For someone who didn't love his wife, this man showed an amazing amount of compassion. "I want to try wiping her face with a cool cloth. If we can get her more comfortable, she might relax."

"Jerusha!" The scream pulled Jerusha back to Sheila's side. Now the young mother was curled in a ball, hugging her knees. Jerusha rubbed her back until she relaxed. She seemed more comfortable on her side, so Jerusha positioned a pillow between her knees and another at her back. She felt a cloth pressed into her hand, but when she looked up, Lewis had already disappeared.

The night passed slowly. At times, the pain would disappear and Sheila would sleep. But just when Jerusha had begun to hope, Sheila would awake with a cry of agony. Jerusha tried to keep the bedclothes smoothed, Sheila's face cooled, and her hair pulled away from her face. It seemed to be all she could do. Lewis kept Jerusha supplied with fresh cloths and hot tea. Jerusha remembered the last time she had worked through the night: the night of the explosion when she'd helped Corporal Sutherland. He might know what to do here. But his absence of late made her reluctant to send for him. Dawn's gray light announced another day in progress and Sheila slept again. Jerusha heard a curious clatter outside the room and tiptoed to investigate.

Lewis had set up a small table with two chairs. Steaming cups of coffee perched beside plates of scrambled eggs and perfectly browned toast. "Thought you might like to eat while she rests," he whispered.

Jerusha smiled her thanks, realizing how hungry she felt. She couldn't believe this man had cooked such a perfect-looking meal.

He seemed to read her thoughts. "I spent almost a year as mother and father both to my boys. I learned." A shadow passed over his face.

In her exhaustion, she spoke before she thought. "Do you still miss her so much?"

His eyes widened in surprise. "Who?"

"Your first wife."

He looked intently at Jerusha for several moments, then his expression softened. "Her death caused me grief, but I had to let go of her long ago. With two small boys and a farm, I had no choice. I actually got used to being alone before God sent me Sheila." His voice took on a note of wonder. "Maggie will always be a special memory, but Sheila's my heart now. I couldn't bear it if—" His voice broke. He strode abruptly out of the house.

Jerusha felt like a sharp blow had taken her breath away. She couldn't believe she had asked such a personal question, and the answer surprised her even more. She recalled the strange words she'd spoken in comfort the night before. "Lewis cares for you." She'd had no idea where they'd come from, but they were more true than she could have guessed. How could Sheila have missed it?

Moans from the bedroom indicated Sheila's agony had awakened her again. This time the pain didn't pause. Shortly after noon, her water broke, sweeping away any hope that the baby might be saved. Jerusha was still trying to change the sheets in between Sheila's spasms when the doctor arrived. When he saw Sheila, his exhaustion dropped like an unwanted blanket, replaced by tense concern.

Lewis appeared and Jerusha heard their whispered conversation outside the room. "I can't do anything for the little one."

"What about my wife?"

"She's had a good nurse, and we'll do what we can from here."

She had no time to relish the praise. Sheila's pain intensified. Jerusha's hands felt crushed from her squeezing. Then quiet moans replaced the screams. Her grip grew less strangling, and she merely moved her legs instead of thrashing across the bed. Jerusha looked at the doctor. Was this good or bad?

The doctor put his face close to Sheila's. "Don't give up, girl. We need your help to do this right. Push."

Was it an hour or minutes later when the tiny stillborn boy appeared? He fit easily in Doctor Pierce's hand. Without a word, Lewis carried his infant son's body from the room.

Jerusha breathed a sigh of relief that the struggle was over. At least for Sheila. Jerusha felt a wave of rising anger. She'd begun to believe God might actually care. *If He honestly loved Sheila, why had He broken her heart?* Maybe He didn't care as much about the details of life as people had led her to believe.

"Towels, quick!" The doctor's shout snapped Jerusha back to reality. A bright red stain spread rapidly under Sheila, who appeared to be sleeping peacefully. Not even knowing where to find towels, Jerusha ran from the room to search for anything that might work.

Lewis met her at the bottom of the stairs, his arms full of the precious linen. "Is she in trouble?"

Jerusha couldn't answer, but he must have seen the answer on her face. He followed her to his wife's side. "How bad is it, Doc?"

"If you've ever prayed, this is the time for it. But make some tea out of this while you're at it. Not too hot, so we can feed it to her." Without looking up, he reached into his bag and handed Lewis a small paper-wrapped package. Lewis ran from the room.

"Let's get her feet up." The doctor reached for pillows and wrapped them in a soiled sheet. Jerusha automatically lifted Sheila's legs.

Lewis returned with the tea. Brushing aside Jerusha's help, he tenderly lifted his wife's head with one hand and held the cup to her lips with the other. "Don't give up on me, love. I need you." He murmured desperately to her until the cup was emptied.

"Good. Be ready to do that again in five minutes. I need more sheets." The doctor fashioned another cushion and placed it under Sheila's hips. He looked at Jerusha. "Keep her warm. The way she's losing blood, she's going to get chilled. We don't need that, too."

The three worked together in a desperate rhythm, replacing linen, making tea, and keeping Sheila's body protected from chill. Jerusha wondered how much longer Sheila could stand the drain. Surely God wouldn't take Lewis' second wife, too.

"I think it's slowing," the doctor finally whispered. "Give her another cup of tea." He and Jerusha watched.

Lewis held another cupful to his wife's lips. "Just a bit, my girl. I'll pour some in, now swallow. Come on, swallow. Sheila, my heart, please swallow. You have to, if you're going to stay with me. Good girl. Now again. Come on, sweetheart, one more time." He set the empty cup on the floor and wrapped both arms around Sheila. "Don't leave me, girl. I need you too much. Our baby's gone. I won't let you go, too." His voice dropped to a broken whisper. "Can you hear me, Sheila? I love you. Please hang on, for my sake. Fight, my girl. Just fight a little bit, and I'll help you do the rest." He buried his face in her damp, tangled hair.

Jerusha had to leave the room. She couldn't remember ever seeing such naked emotion. Its intensity brought tears to her eyes. Could God's love be anything like it?

ten

With Lewis by her side, Sheila pulled through the night. For the next twenty-four hours, Jerusha and Dr. Pierce alternated their watch, while Lewis refused to move. By the third day after Jerusha had been summoned, the doctor declared their patient out of danger.

"But she still needs lots of rest. I'd like you to stay on here for awhile, Miss Porter, that is if Lewis doesn't mind." The doctor looked from one to the other.

"I'd be grateful if you could." The farmer looked appealingly at Jerusha.

She thought of David and the piles of laundry. "I'd like to, but—"

The doctor cut her off. "Would you let me talk with the reverend about it? I know you have responsibilities in town, but I'd feel a lot better if there were another woman here to keep an eye on Mrs. Murray."

Jerusha nodded her consent. It felt strange, the intensity of her desire to stay. She hadn't even considered what the proper response might be. She simply wanted to do whatever she could to help this couple she suddenly cared about deeply.

"I'll be back this afternoon, then." The doctor lifted his hat to Jerusha, then turned to Lewis. "Your prescription for today is at least four hours' sleep. Anything you think needs doing can wait." A blast of cold air filled the room as he opened the door, and they heard his pickup rumble to life.

Lewis rubbed his puffy eyes. "I guess I'm under doctor's orders. You'll call if she wakes up?"

"I promise." She felt limp from tension and lack of sleep.

He shook his head wearily. "I don't know what I would have done if we'd lost her."

"But we didn't, Lewis. Just go sleep, please." She didn't realize until he started upstairs that she'd used his first name. It had just seemed right. In fact, formal address would have been insulting after what they'd experienced together.

Sheila still slept soundly. Jerusha pulled a chair from the kitchen into the bedroom. Maybe she could catch a light nap. Sitting up, she shouldn't sleep soundly enough to miss something if Sheila awoke.

Midafternoon dusk had already darkened the outdoors when Jerusha opened her eyes. It took her a few moments to recall why she'd fallen asleep here. Her shoulders and neck ached from the awkward position in which she'd slept. She looked over at the bed in time to see Sheila's eyes flutter open.

"Jerusha?" Her voice was a weak whisper.

"I'm glad you're awake." Jerusha couldn't tell how much of the past two days Sheila remembered, or what she needed to hear.

Sheila stretched out a hand trembling from weakness. "I'm glad you're here. I feel so tired."

Jerusha tried to smile reassuringly. "You've had a difficult time."

"The baby?" Sheila's eyes filled.

Jerusha instinctively folded her into a hug. "You're going to be okay."

Sheila's sobs were little more than mild tremors, but Jerusha could feel her grief. Eventually, the young mother quieted enough to ask another question. "Lewis?"

"He's been worried sick about you." Jerusha pulled back to look into Sheila's eyes. "He went half crazy when we almost lost you."

"Was he in here with me?"

"Yes, from Saturday night until this morning."

"Did he hold me?"

Jerusha only nodded.

"I remember hearing him begging me not to leave him. I think he told me he loves me. Did he really?" Sheila's eyes lit with hope even though her voice had faded to the softest of whispers.

"Yes. He was really frightened for you." Tears filled Jerusha's eyes at the memory. "Don't try to talk anymore. Just rest. I'll bring you some soup."

Sheila seemed to slip back into sleep, a smile hovering around her pale lips. Jerusha opened a jar of canned chicken, then added some water to make a light broth for her friend's next meal. A creak on the stairs turned her attention from the stove. Lewis descended the stairs slowly, his hair and clothing still rumpled from sleep. He looked questioningly at her.

Jerusha didn't have to ask what he meant. "She woke up a few minutes ago, but I think she's sleeping again."

"Did she say anything?"

"She asked about the baby."

"You told her?"

"She guessed. She doesn't know it was a boy." Jerusha wondered how much to tell this bearded man who, just a week ago, had been little more than a stranger. "Lewis?"

He'd been headed toward Sheila's room, but he turned back.

"Maybe this isn't my place, but I think I need to tell you something."

He nodded understanding and pulled out a chair near the table.

Jerusha twisted a towel in her hands, afraid she was making a mistake, yet compelled to let him in on what she knew. "Remember when Sheila came to help me with laundry right after the explosion?"

He nodded again.

"She told Maisie and I then she really wanted this baby to be a boy." She paused, not knowing how to continue.

"Why?" Lewis' voice was a ragged whisper.

She studied the twisted towel. "She hoped it would make you love her." Once the words were out, she could look at his eyes.

He moved his mouth, but made no sound. Tears ran down into his beard. Finally he croaked, "Do you know why?"

As had happened last night, her answer seemed to come from nowhere, words that gripped her heart while they appeared to touch the feelings of the man across from her. "Some people just have a hard time feeling loved, no matter what others tell them." Could that be why she couldn't find God's love? Maybe it was there, just like Lewis' had been for Sheila, but she hadn't believed it.

"What do I do? How do I convince her how precious she is? If I'd lost her..." He buried his face in his hands.

"I know." She surprised herself by putting a hand on his arm, knowing he needed the comfort of physical contact. "She remembers you holding her last night, begging her not to die. Maybe she needs to be held again so she doesn't think it was a dream."

Lewis laid one of his roughened hands on hers. "Thanks, Jerusha." He rubbed his thumb across his eyes. "I think I'll get cleaned up so I'm not so grubby when she wakes up."

When Dr. Pierce arrived, his face had lost its haggard exhaustion. "You look like you've rested a bit," he greeted Jerusha. "I talked to your brother and he says he can manage fine if you want to stay for awhile."

"What about the laundry?"

The doctor chuckled. "The reverend said you'd ask, and said to tell you Miss Clarke and Mrs. Barry have volunteered to take care of things for as long as you have to be gone. It seems word of the trouble out here spread quickly."

Jerusha could barely believe her ears. It sounded as if they wanted to help her as much as she wanted to help Lewis and Sheila. "That's good of them," she said lamely.

"You and the reverend have put a lot of caring into this town. I figure it's time you got some back." He cleared his throat roughly. "Where's Lewis?"

The voice spoke from the stairs. "Right here." With clean, combed hair and fresh clothing, he looked almost like a different person.

"Isn't it amazing what a nap and a bath can do for a man?" The doctor laughed. "You look a thousand times better. This morning I wasn't sure you'd make it."

Lewis shook the doctor's hand. "Thanks for being here."

"I'm glad I was. How's our patient?"

"She woke up a bit earlier, then went right back to sleep," Jerusha explained. "I've got some broth ready for the next time she wakes up."

"She probably won't be awake much over the next few days, which is just right. Warm broth is the perfect food. Any kind of hot liquids she wants are fine, but go easy on the solid food for awhile. I'll go take a look." He followed Lewis down the hall.

Jerusha finished putting the broth on to simmer, then began peeling vegetables for an evening meal. The doctor didn't linger in Sheila's room.

"I assume you're willing to stay for awhile?" he asked, accepting a cup of coffee.

Jerusha nodded.

"Good. They're both going to need you, especially when the boys come home. Sheila's not out of the woods yet, and the least bit of overexertion could start the bleeding again. I don't want her even out of bed for two weeks. Lewis is so relieved she's still alive he doesn't realize yet how long it will take her to recover." He blew on his coffee for a few moments. "He tells me she asked you about the baby."

"She knows he's...that he didn't make it." Jerusha tried to swallow back the tears.

"I think she's going to have a rough time adjusting. I don't mind telling you I've rarely seen a woman as distraught as she was when I first got here."

"She'd calmed quite a bit by then."

"That's what I was afraid of. It's going to take a lot of love to pull her through. She's a believer, isn't she?"

The question surprised her. "Yes. She told me once she wouldn't have made it to Canada without God."

"She's going to need reminding of His love." He smiled at Jerusha's wide-eyed surprise. "That's an unusual prescription, isn't it? But I can't imagine doctoring in these parts without Him. We all need Him for whatever we have to do, I guess. Well, I'd best be on my way. Please tell Lewis I'll be back tomorrow."

Jerusha felt stunned by his comments. It seemed like every direction she turned, she was reminded of a love she still wasn't sure of. She'd like to ask Keith about it, if he ever showed up again.

Life slowly settled into routine. Lewis brought his boys

home Tuesday morning. Jerusha found herself longing for the ease of her laundry business after three days keeping track of Colin and Bradley. Colin was five and Bradley, three. Rarely a morning or afternoon passed without one of them creating a mess somewhere, usually involving a fresh change of clothing. She barely had time to clean up from one meal before it was time to prepare another, not to mention endless loads of laundry and an infinite number of questions.

"Where are birds in the winter?" from Colin, who seemed fascinated by the seasons.

"Why is the stove hot?" from Bradley, whose favorite questions always began with why.

"When does spring come?"

"Where is your mommy?"

"Does the snow go away in spring or summer?"

"Why can't cows feed themselves?"

Despite the frustrations, she found herself developing an affection for the boys. She had always thought of herself as awkward around children, but Colin and Bradley didn't give her time to be uncomfortable. After a couple of days, they weren't content to go to bed until they had hugged Daddy, Mommy, and "Auntie 'Rusha." She had no words for the delight their enthusiastic love brought her.

Caring for Sheila proved to be a light load. Lewis did his chores in record time, spending every available minute with his wife, whether she was sleeping or awake. Every time Jerusha went to do something for her friend, she found the job already done and Lewis sitting on the bed holding Sheila in his arms as she rested. Sheila's eyes took on a shine Jerusha had never seen before. Though she cried periodically over her baby, she didn't encounter the despair Dr. Pierce had feared.

One of their rare moments together came when Sheila asked to have her hair washed. "I want to be fresh and as pretty as I can when Lewis comes back from feeding the livestock," she explained. Then while Jerusha brushed out the wet locks, she quietly commented, "This sounds terrible, but Davey's death may have been good for me."

"What do you mean?" Jerusha had been wondering how her friend felt about the loss of the son she had wanted so desperately.

"I thought a son would make Lewis love me. If Davey had lived, I might never have believed Lewis loves me for myself. But what I felt was my failure has been what I needed to enable me to see how much he cares. His love is almost too good to be true."

"It's for real, all right." Jerusha recalled again the agony in Lewis' eyes as the three of them had struggled together to stop Sheila's bleeding. She helped settle her friend back against the pillows, her clean hair spread out behind her head.

"Hmmm. This feels good. I didn't do anything, and I'm still tuckered out." Sheila snuggled under the comforter and closed her eyes.

Jerusha tucked the blankets in around the edge of the bed to prevent drafts. "Dr. Pierce says it will take you awhile to get your strength back."

Sheila opened her eyes a bit. "Thanks for being here, Jerusha."

"I wouldn't want to be anywhere else." She intended to reassure her friend, but the words she chose surprised her. Amazingly enough, she really was doing exactly what she wanted to do.

eleven

Bradley and Colin had finally settled down for their naps, much to Jerusha's relief. Sheila was now strong enough to move from the bedroom to the sitting room, though she often tried to do more. Once the boys fell asleep, Sheila would also rest, and Jerusha would be able to catch up on bread baking and the ever-present laundry. She measured milk, honey, and yeast, then stirred in the flour. A few minutes of kneading and she could put the bread to rise on the far corner of the stove while she washed a couple loads of work clothes and little boys' play clothes. Good thing there weren't diapers to rinse, too. Jerusha smiled at her thoughts. A month ago, diapers would have been the furthest thing from her mind. These two small boys had entwined themselves in her heart, making her wonder what it would be like to have sons of her own. A sharp rap on the door startled her. She looked quickly out the window, but only saw a green army jeep. Could it be? But why would he come all the way out here?

She opened the door to greet the face that had intruded on her thoughts all too often in the past month. "Corporal Sutherland! Come in."

His eyebrows pulled together and he growled something under his breath. By the time he shed his parka and stepped out of his boots, his face had cleared. "Your brother told me I'd find you here. Word has it you've been doing a great job of being both nurse and mother."

The heat spreading across her face had little to do with her proximity to the cook stove. "You're not looking for Lewis? He's out in the barn."

"I'm glad he's outside, because that means you have to visit with me. You look like you're enjoying being out here."

"I am." The statement seemed too terse, but she didn't know how else to explain her feelings.

His gaze became more intent. "Your eyes look brighter and happier than I've ever seen them. I'm glad."

She silently handed him a cup of steaming coffee and a piece of last night's leftover cake, not sure what to say next.

"Thanks." He grinned and took a large bite of cake. "The cooks sure don't produce anything like this at the chow hall. I hear you had a close call with your patient."

Jerusha nodded. "I wished for you to be here."

"Why? I'm just a medic, not a doctor." His eyes widened in surprise.

"I'm neither and Dr. Pierce was busy delivering a healthy baby over by Rolla."

"You honestly thought of me?" His smile indicated he was teasing, but his gaze probed hers intently.

"I've thought of you a lot in the last month. I was afraid I'd offended you." She studied the wood grain of the table.

"Offended me? How?"

His shocked tone pulled her gaze back to his face. "When we were skiing and I wouldn't answer your question about God. I'm not the kind of Christian you are."

"Wait just a minute." He set his cup on the table with a thump. "Are you saying you think I didn't come visit because I was upset with you?"

She nodded, wondering why she'd even opened the subject.

"I'm really sorry." His voice dropped to comforting softness. "I was out of town. I get sent up the road periodically to relieve other medics further north. They shipped me out the day after the skiing party, and I just got back this morning. I'm so accustomed to the way the army works I never dreamed you wouldn't know. Can you forgive me?"

She smiled, wondering why she suddenly felt so much lighter, almost like dancing across the kitchen. Instead, she refilled his coffee cup and reached for the bread bowl. "I'm glad it wasn't me. What's it like up the highway?"

He watched her sprinkle flour, then dump the bread dough on the table. "Pretty rough. They're trying to hack this highway out of frozen ground, and most of the troops have never encountered this kind of cold. There's lots of frostbite and injuries from guys trying to work without gloves. Their hands get cold and clumsy real quick. Or should I say very quickly. I'm picking up soldier talk."

"I've never understood what this project is all about anyway. Why does the American army need to build a Canadian road?"

"That could be a loaded question. We need to get supplies to an American army base in Alaska."

The bread dough was getting sticky, so she sprinkled more flour and continued kneading. "I didn't know there was one there."

His mouth tightened. "There isn't, but we're trying to get one there as fast as we can. That's why we need the road."

"What's the rush?"

"Does the name Pearl Harbor mean anything to you?"

"Isn't that where the Japanese made a vicious attack on the Americans?"

"That's it. The Japanese have been basically cleaning up on us ever since. Before we know it, we could find them on our shores."

"Like here in Canada?" She knew little about the Japanese, but she'd always heard the word uttered with tones of dread.

"Could be. We're doing our best to fight them back, but we haven't been too successful so far."

"And this new road is supposed to help?" She couldn't figure out how a trail hacked through the wilderness could make any difference in a war between foreigners.

He slid his chair back and stood. "We're hoping it will help us at least prepare for an attack on this continent, if not launch one ourselves. And speaking of attacks, I'd better get back to base, or my CO will launch one on me." His grin looked just like Colin's when Lewis tried scolding him. "Thanks for the cake."

She wanted to ask when he'd be back, but the question felt improper. She settled for, "I'm glad you stopped by."

With another charming grin, he slipped into his parka and boots and left only a blast of cold air and an empty coffee cup as evidence of his visit.

To her surprise, he dropped by the next day, and the next. By the time Jerusha had been with the Murrays for a month, he'd become a regular visitor, usually around supper time.

"I've heard you army guys'll do anything for a home-cooked meal, but a twenty-minute drive?" Lewis teased one evening, handing the corporal a plateful of hot stew.

Corporal Sutherland only raised his eyebrows innocently in reply, then winked at Jerusha. She focused on getting the boys' plates filled and cooled, while their chatter eliminated what could have been an awkward silence.

"Are you really a soldier?"

He smiled at young Colin's enthusiasm. "No, I just take care of hurt soldiers."

"So you don't shoot people?" The boy was clearly disappointed.

"No, son, and I'm glad."

"Why?"

"'Cause I don't like hurting people."

Now Bradley jumped in. "But if they're bad guys it doesn't matter."

Corporal Sutherland looked at Lewis, who only shrugged his shoulders, indicating he, too, waited for the corporal's reply. "It's like this, boys. Does Jesus love everybody or just a few people?"

There it was again—God's love out in the open where Jerusha couldn't ignore it. She mashed harder on Bradley's vegetables.

"Everybody." Colin proudly declared.

"So if I love Jesus, should I love everybody or just the people I like?"

Colin's enthusiasm was waning. "I guess everybody."

"Do you kill people you love?" Corporal Sutherland's manner remained gentle, even though he emphasized the point.

Bradley knew the answer to that one. "My mommy says Jesus wants us to be kind to ev'body."

"That's right, Bradley. That's why I only help hurt people. I guess I'm not a real soldier."

"But you're nice, anyway," Colin assured him. "That's what my mommy told Daddy."

The adults laughed, each self-conscious for a different

reason. "How about eating, boys," Lewis suggested, with the father tone of voice that left no room for discussion. "If Mommy's still awake when you get finished, we'll go in and talk to her for awhile."

Jerusha recognized the blatant scheme to leave her alone with the corporal. For some reason, she felt almost grateful for it.

"How's Mrs. Lewis doing?" Corporal Sutherland asked quietly when the other three left.

"Better than the doctor predicted." She didn't know how much to tell. If she started talking about Sheila and Lewis' marriage, she'd probably stumble into her own still uncertain feelings about God.

"Sometimes tragedy carries wonderful discoveries with it." He stacked dishes and brought them to the cupboard, where she filled wash basins with hot water. "You're surprised I said that."

His perception made her nervous. "I just wondered how you guessed."

"We men are more observant than you think." He smiled teasingly, then sobered. "It just seemed to me Mrs. Lewis worked pretty hard at trying to please someone who already thinks she's wonderful. Kind of like we do with God sometimes."

His comment touched too close to her feelings. She concentrated on cleaning the stack of dishes, waiting for him to change the subject.

He pulled a chair close to where she worked. "You know, Miss Porter, you never did answer my question at the skiing party. Have you thought any more about it?"

She looked directly into the gray eyes watching her with such concern. "I've thought of little else. No sooner do I think I've found an answer than something happens to make me lose it."

"Want to talk to an old soldier about it?"

"Actually, David and I were discussing it a bit when Lewis came to get me." She took a deep breath for courage, then related David's comments that evening and her own feelings. "The verse Mrs. Barry read made me think maybe I haven't understood God at all. It seems to say He loves us no matter what we do. But that just doesn't make sense."

"Why not?"

"If He's so perfect and holy, how can He love such imperfect people?"

"Because He's God."

She looked at him in confusion while she wiped biscuit crumbs off the table.

"Let's try it from this angle. If we have to be perfect in order to be loved by Him, then what was Jesus' death all about?"

She had never thought about that. In recent years, Calvary had become a religious historical event, without any personal meaning. She remembered the verse which had started this train of thought: "...while we were yet sinners, Christ died for us." There seemed to be a comforting message there, if she could only hear it through the confusion of her own thoughts.

"Jerusha." His gentle voice drew her gaze to his face. "It seems to me you're trying to figure God out. Faith is simply accepting that He is who He says He is."

"But the God you talk about is so different from what I've always thought He is! Sometimes it just doesn't make sense."

"I feel if I could explain God, He wouldn't be God anymore, just a creation of my imagination. What makes Him so wonderful is that He's Who He is, yet He chooses to love us finite, imperfect humans."

She shook her head at him. "I wish I could feel the way you do."

Whatever she had been planning to say further was cut off by the attack of a small body. "'Night, Auntie 'Rusha."

"Good night, Bradley." She detached his arms from around her legs and picked him up for a tight hug. "You could have called me from upstairs."

"But Daddy said not to 'sturb you. I thinked if I comed in here, I wouldn't 'sturb you, but you'd hafta hug me."

She kissed the boy's soft cheek. "Where's Colin?"

"Here." A quiet whisper came from the stairs. "I couldn't sleep without a good night hug."

She carried Bradley to the stairs and hugged his older brother. "Didn't your Daddy hug you?"

"Yeah, but I wanted one from you."

"Boys!" Lewis called from Sheila's room. "I thought I sent you upstairs."

"Auntie 'Rusha wanted to hug us. We didn't 'sturb her, Daddy," Bradley explained quickly.

Lewis approached the stairs, the twinkle in his eye indicating he guessed what had really happened. "Ok, now git!"

"Kids are special, aren't they?" the corporal commented when she returned.

"At least those two are." She grinned self-consciously while rinsing the last few dishes. "They've found a soft spot in me I didn't know I had."

"I noticed it the night of the explosion. As soon as you

picked up that hurt boy, a new gentleness showed. I like it." His smile seemed almost intimate.

She sought for safer conversational ground. "Have you been around children much?"

"My sisters each have three, and I love spoiling all of them. After the war ends, I hope God allows me to have my own family." Unfamiliar shadows darkened his eyes.

She studied his face. This was an unfamiliar side of him. "Why wait for the war?" She hoped the impulsive question wasn't offensively personal.

He sat silent for so long she wondered if he'd decided not to answer. She set a cup of hot coffee on the counter beside him, then pulled a chair closer to the stove—and to him.

"I'd never ask any woman to marry an army man."

If she thought before she spoke, she would have bitten her next inquiry back. "Why?" Then good manners took over. Her face heated. "I'm sorry. I shouldn't pry."

He reassured her with a brief smile. "Remember I told you the other day about the base in Alaska? That's supposed to be a jumping-off place for an offensive into Japan. As soon as the Alcan Highway is complete, I could get shipped up there and then maybe to Japan. It would be unfair to leave a wife and children behind to wonder if I'd ever come home again."

The thought of him leaving never to return left a little cold spot in her middle. *Surely God wouldn't permit someone who loved Him so much to be killed! But then Sheila's baby hadn't even had a chance to decide for or against God.* She studied his sober expression, usually so cheerful. "Does it bother you to think about God letting you get killed?"

Surprise covered his face. "I'm doing what I feel He wants me to do, so it's up to Him whether or not I survive. Why do you ask?"

"If He really loves you, why wouldn't He keep you safe?" she whispered, not sure how her friend would respond. Maybe even God would be offended by the thought.

The corporal sat silently for several minutes. "I wish I could explain why God allows the things He does. Like this war. He could have prevented it, but that would have meant overriding the wills of men and nations. People being hurt and killed is part of war. All I know for sure is that He is God, and He's in charge."

Jerusha couldn't make sense of his gentle words. The familiar resentment churned in her stomach again. She thought of her often-absent parents, pursuing God's will while she cried herself to sleep at night. Her own attempts to follow God's will had dumped her in this revolting boom town.

"Jerusha?" the corporal called softly. When she looked at him, he continued. "This isn't really about what might or might not happen to me, is it?"

Jerusha wiped the clean counter again to avoid his gaze.

He wouldn't let her shut him out. "Would you mind telling me what God's done to make you question Him so harshly?"

Again, she felt punched in the stomach. "What makes you think that?"

"Your anger at Him is written all over your face." The words carried no hint of accusation. "Will you tell me why?"

She whirled to face him, feeling like the lid to her seething emotions had been pried off. "My parents have been missionaries all my life. All I've heard about them is how wonderful, how dedicated, they are. When they'd come home on furlough, I'd try to be as good as I knew how so they'd love me enough to want to stay. But they always went back, usually sooner than they'd planned, because they said God needed them. Why didn't God realize I needed them, too? If He loved me, He sure had a strange way of showing it." To her dismay, tears poured down her face.

He merely held his arms out to her, tears glistening in his eyes. When she didn't move, he took a couple of slow steps toward her until he was close enough to embrace her. His hug broke the last fragments of her reserve. She sobbed into his shirt front, feeling like a small girl again. Years of grief and anger poured through her tears. He simply held her close, saying nothing until her shoulders stopped shaking.

"Every time they left, it felt like personal rejection, didn't it?"

The rumble in his chest as he spoke brought as much comfort as his words. She nodded against him, wondering why she'd never been able to describe her feelings so well.

"Rushi, God never asked them to choose between Him and you." Large hands rubbed her neck and shoulders. "His will isn't some arbitrary decision He makes without regard for our feelings or the feelings of those we love. I can't explain why God allowed things to happen in your family the way He did, just like I don't know why God allowed Sheila's baby to come so early. But I do know He's hurt with you all this time, just like He's cried with Sheila and Lewis."

She pulled back to look into his face. "But I've blamed Him for everything!"

"Some of Jesus' best friends did the same thing. When

Lazarus died, the first thing his sisters said to Jesus was, 'If you'd been here, this wouldn't have happened.' He didn't defend Himself or try to explain anything. In fact, the Apostle John said He saw their grief and was troubled. He shared their grief, even though He knew He would raise Lazarus to life." He rested his hands lightly on her shoulders. "He doesn't expect us to be stoic. He knows we'll weep and rant at Him. He just waits until we're ready to listen so He can show us all over again how much He loves us."

Jerusha felt half-ashamed of the question, but she had to ask. "Why doesn't He at least tell us why He lets things happen the way they do?"

Keith's eyes softened with a compassionate smile. "I don't know, Rushi. Lots of people in Scripture asked Him to explain Himself."

"What did He say?"

"Most often, He simply showed them Himself."

The warmth of his hands on her shoulders suddenly felt too personal. She moved away, studying his face for clues to the mystery. "You mean He never told them why, and they just decided everything was all right?"

"Any revelation of God includes His love. When they saw God as He revealed Himself to them, they realized He can do nothing outside His fathomless love for us, the people He's created for fellowship with Him. His love is the essence of who He is, which enables us to love Him in return. When we know His love, we don't need explanations."

"I wish I could." She shook her head sadly, looking away from him. The darkness outside the kitchen window looked like what she felt inside.

"You will."

"How do you know?"

"Because since the night of the explosion, I've been asking Him to make it so."

twelve

The next day, Dr. Pierce gave permission for Sheila to start taking up the care of her household again. "But go carefully, now, Mrs. Murray. At least one nap every day, and don't lift anything, not even your sons."

Jerusha expected to see pain on Sheila's face at the reference to her sons. The children under discussion were actually her stepsons. Her own son lay in a shallow grave already covered by a snowbank. Instead, Sheila gave Lewis a glowing look and turned back to the doctor. "My guardian angels here don't give me a chance to misbehave." She smiled at Jerusha. "I haven't even been allowed to wash my own hair."

"Which is as it should be," Dr. Pierce pronounced. "I know I'm leaving you in expert hands." He reached for his coat and bag. Lewis remained behind with his wife, but Jerusha followed the doctor. His hand was on the door when she finally found the courage to address him.

"Dr. Pierce, I need to ask you a question, if you have time."

He immediately put his bag on the floor. "I have all the time you need. What is it?"

Her discomfort increased, but she knew she felt driven to find answers. "You mentioned that Sheila might have a hard time adjusting to her baby's death."

He nodded, watching her with kindly brown eyes.

"She hasn't. Is she just pretending to be okay, or is there

something I've missed?"

"Have you asked her about it?"

"No. I've had little time alone with her. Lewis hovers around her like a mosquito in the dark."

"What a romantic simile." The doctor chuckled. "But I know what you mean, and it could be the answer to your question. Maybe just realizing she's loved provided the healing she needed."

Jerusha shook her head. "It doesn't make sense."

"Love often doesn't, Miss Porter. God's love is incomprehensible, and human love is supposed to be a reflection of Him. I'd recommend you talk with Mrs. Murray. Since she's experienced it, she might be able to help you understand." He pulled his hat flaps down over his ears, picked up his bag, and departed in a gust of chilly air.

Jerusha puttered around the kitchen, wiping clean counters, straightening tidy cupboards, stoking an already-crackling fire. Anything to avoid talking with Sheila just now. Should she face her friend immediately, Sheila would be able to see her conflict. Somehow it didn't seem right for a person of Jerusha's background to be struggling so intensely with the love of the One she proclaimed to serve. She heard Lewis' clumping steps coming from the bedroom.

"I'll probably be out until supper time," he said from beside the door, where he donned layer after layer of warm clothing. "Now that my wife's on the mend, I need to get caught up out in the barn. I'd like to be able to be on hand for the first couple of weeks after you leave." His lips twitched in the half-smile that was Lewis Murray's version of a grin.

His expression lingered in her memory while she peeled

vegetables to add to the roast already cooking. Lewis could easily seem unfriendly, even surly. She'd never seen him grin like Keith, much less laugh. He didn't talk easily, either. Now that she had spent time around him and his family, she knew his gentleness expressed itself in his actions rather than his words. If one watched closely, hints of his emotions showed in his eyes—brightening for his sons, softening for his wife. What a contrast to Sheila's easy expression of her feelings! Could her feeling unloved have been no more than not understanding Lewis' ways of communicating? A scuffling sound from the direction of Sheila's bedroom interrupted her thoughts. She plopped the last handful of carrots in the roasting pan and hurried to investigate.

Sheila looked up guiltily as Jerusha peered into the room. "I'm staying warm," she announced from where she stood next to the partially made bed.

Jerusha duly noted the quilted robe encasing her friend from shoulders to ankles. The scuffling sounds had come from Sheila's rabbit-fur moccasins as she had moved from one side of the bed to the other, straightening the covers. A pile of linen near the door indicated Sheila had changed the sheets before being discovered. Jerusha tried to look stern. "Dr. Pierce said no lifting."

"Sheets aren't heavy."

"But it's hard work tucking them around the edge of the mattress. Why didn't you ask for help?"

Sheila beamed. "It just feels so good to be out of bed!"

"If you're not careful, you'll end up right back there and Lewis will have my hide!"

Sheila giggled delightedly. "It's so wonderfully fragile and carefully cherished he makes me feel." She lowered herself back onto the bed. "I do need to sit and catch my breath a bit."

Jerusha studied her carefully. Somehow she looked years younger than she had even a couple of months ago. After her harrowing experience, she should still look drained and tired, or at the very least, sad.

Suddenly it felt like the perfect time for questions. "What's made the difference, Sheila?"

She didn't pretend not to understand. "All the hours Lewis spent with me right after the baby came showed me how many faces love wears. I kept looking for words and completely missed Lewis' more subtle ways of caring. Lying here, I had nothing but time to watch him and think. Now I know what to look for, I see his love for me in everything he does."

"But what about the baby?"

Sheila's face shadowed. "What do you mean?"

"Maybe I shouldn't have brought it up." Jerusha backed toward the door.

"Don't be afraid to talk about him, Jerusha. He's still my baby, and I still wish I could have held him and watched him grow." Tears misted her eyes, though she smiled encouragingly.

"You wanted him so badly. Even Dr. Pierce predicted you might have a hard time adjusting."

Sheila leaned back against the pillows. "I've cried lots." Drops sliding down her cheeks verified her statement. "But so has Lewis, and somehow that makes it easier. He loves me so much he's willing to hurt with me. We've become best friends since we lost the baby. I'm not glad Davey died. But if he hadn't, I might never have discovered what his daddy is really like." Now Sheila studied Jerusha. "It's hard to understand, isn't it?"

Jerusha nodded. She still couldn't see the baby's death as anything less than tragedy.

"It's kind of like my relationship with God," Sheila continued quietly. "He always seemed remote to me until life got hard after my Ma died. I'd cry myself to sleep at night, and I'd feel His presence in my dreams. The seamstress I worked for would scream at me, and I'd feel inside me how much God loved me in spite of the horrible things she said. And coming over on the ship, when I felt like I'd die from either fright or sickness, I knew He'd take care of me. I guess it takes the difficult times to make me sensitive enough to realize what He's really like." Gentle silence followed.

"I think I smell the roast burning." Jerusha hurried to the kitchen, glad for an excuse to escape the mood created by Sheila's words. She'd barely closed the oven door when pattering feet on the stairs announced the boys' awakening from their afternoon naps. Shuffling slowly, Sheila met them at the bottom.

"Mama!" they chorused, delight shining in their big brown eyes.

Jerusha watched carefully as Sheila hugged the boys, then guided them to the rocker in the sitting room. "Colin, if you'd fetch me a book, we can read a story. Bradley, pull up that stool for you and one on the other side for Colin."

"But I want to sit on your lap." Bradley's lower lip trembled convincingly as he lifted a sad gaze to his mother's face.

Well accustomed to his clever theatrics, Jerusha intervened before Sheila's tender heart overrode common sense.

She hurried to kneel beside the boy. "Bradley, your daddy needs you to help take care of your mommy for awhile."

"She doesn't look sick." Curiosity replaced Bradley's pout.

"That's because her hurt is inside her body where we can't see it. But if she does things the doctor said not to do, it could make her even more sick. That would make your daddy very sad." Jerusha glanced at Sheila, whose eyes twinkled with merriment.

Bradley looked seriously at Jerusha, then at his mother, as if to verify Jerusha's comments. "Did the doctor tell her not to hold me?"

Jerusha nodded solemnly.

"And if she does, Daddy might spank her for dis'bedience, right?"

Again she nodded, trying to keep laughter from escaping. From the corner of her eye, she could see Sheila's arms shaking with suppressed giggles.

Colin returned just in time to hear his younger brother's comment. "Daddy wouldn't spank Mommy, silly! They're adults, and adults don't get spankings."

Bradley looked back at Jerusha. "Then what will happen if she holds me?"

Colin knew that answer, too. "You'll get spanked, 'cause Daddy already told us not even to ask her. She's sick and we have to take good care of her so she gets well again."

"I guess that settles it, then." Sheila opened the book, and the boys settled on either side.

After a couple of stories, they were ready to go outside to play. Sheila and Jerusha helped them into heavy pants, sweaters, mitts, hats, and coats, then wrapped scarves snugly around each face.

"They won't be out more than twenty minutes before they'll be wanting in again," Sheila laughed, watching through the window as they tumbled over each other in the snow like a couple of puppies. "While they're out, would you help me do my hair?" When Jerusha nodded, she released the lightly twisted bun at the back of her head. "I want tonight to be a special supper to celebrate my getting well. Moose roast is Lewis' favorite meal, and I'll make him an apple pie when I finish with my hair."

"How about letting me handle the pie?" Jerusha suggested, wrapping a heated towel around Sheila's shoulders. Over the weeks of Sheila's recovery, they had devised a system for getting her hair cleaned quickly, yet thoroughly. Sheila lay across her bed facing the ceiling, her long hair hanging into a small washtub Jerusha had set on a stool.

"This is a lot easier now you're able to help." Jerusha used a cup to pour the warm water through the dark, curly hair.

Sheila's voice softened. "I haven't told you how much I appreciate you coming out here. Lewis has mentioned often how we couldn't have made it through this without you."

The praise made Jerusha uncomfortable. "I'm glad to be able to help, though you and Lewis would have survived fine without me. You're both strong people."

Sheila turned her head abruptly to look into Jerusha's face. "Part of what makes us strong, Jerusha, is having friends like you."

Jerusha concentrated on working lather into the ends of the hair close to Sheila's scalp, then carefully rinsing away the suds. She wrapped a towel around the wet hair, helping Sheila to sit up.

Sheila watched her carry out the washtub, then the stool.

Still silently, she let Jerusha comb out her wet hair. The job was almost finished when she commented, "You've changed since you've been out here. In a good way, I mean."

The comment caught Jerusha completely off guard. "Wh-wh-what do you mean?"

"Like your joking this afternoon with Bradley. Three months ago, you hardly even spoke to the boys. You've handled them like family lately."

"I guess being around them so much has made me more comfortable with them."

"And maybe love is teaching you not to be afraid of being yourself."

Jerusha dropped the comb with a gasp. "Love?"

"You've had little part of a real family, haven't you?" Sheila asked gently.

Jerusha thought immediately of Uncle Cam and Aunt Vivienne. "My aunt and uncle were like parents to us since our own were overseas so much."

"But you've always seemed to me to be trying to live up to someone else's expectations of you. You've been afraid to let anyone know you or love you just as you are. That's what I've found so wonderful about children. Their little minds are too busy discovering the world to worry about what other people think. They either love people or they don't. It's quite a compliment that our two have fallen so hard for you. They're going to miss you when you go back."

Jerusha visualized the tidy parsonage, unruffled by crying, scattered toys, or spilled food. "I'll miss them, too."

"I'll bring them around lots so you don't forget what love is like. I imagine that army fellow will also do his part."

Voices at the front door rescued Jerusha from reply. "Can we come in now, Auntie 'Rusha? It's cold."

She hurried out to help the two snow-covered figures. "Yes, but shut the door so your mommy doesn't catch a chill." She hung the now wet winter clothing on chairs around the kitchen stove to dry while she made the pie. The smell of cinnamon and apple had begun to fill the house when Sheila finally came out of her room again, fully dressed this time.

"How do I look?" She twirled in front of the stove.

Jerusha tried to look stern. "You look like you've put in a lot of work. Sit down."

Sheila sat, eyes glowing. "But do I look like an invalid?"

"Definitely not." Jerusha hugged her, then backed up to look at her again. Sheila had braided her dark hair in a coronet around her head, then donned a soft pink dress with a gathered skirt and a high ruffled neck. The full sleeves ended in ruffles at the wrists. The pink in her dress emphasized the returning glow in her cheeks and deepened the color in her shining eyes. "I think you'll take his breath away."

"Good. Now, would you mind getting the fancy dishes off the top shelf? I'll see if I can find the lacy tablecloth in the linen closet."

Jerusha stopped her with a firm hand on her shoulder. "I don't mind if you sit here and give orders. The best way to end up back in bed is to do too much your first day up."

Sheila sighed in resignation, but the twinkle in her eyes didn't disappear. "Okay, boss. Can you find the dishes?"

In a remarkably short amount of time, the simple kitchen table had been transformed into a dining area fit for Winnipeg's finest home. Under Sheila's direction, Jerusha had also found two hand-carved candle holders and two store-bought pale pink candles. The china had a fine, pink-flowered design enhanced by the lacy tablecloth. Then Sheila sent the boys upstairs for specific pants and shirts "so we can look extra-special nice for Daddy tonight." Neither child looked excited about dressing up, but the novelty of having Mommy help encouraged cooperation.

"Now you," Sheila announced, looking at Jerusha. "I don't want you looking like our kitchen maid."

"But I didn't bring any fancy clothes with me," she protested.

"Which is why it's a good thing we're much the same size. Come with me. The pie won't burn if you hurry."

Feeling helplessly caught in the tide of Sheila's enthusiasm, Jerusha followed. Sheila reached toward a wooden peg behind the curtain that hid hers and Lewis' clothes from view. "I made this while still in Ireland, but the color doesn't suit me. I think it will look marvelous on you." She held up a dress made from a soft woolen fabric the color of Aunt Vivienne's darkest roses. Jerusha had never thought of wearing any color other than "discreet" browns, grays, and blues, but she now wanted nothing more than to try on this beautiful garment. Cloth-covered buttons closed the dress from the waist up to a wide collar. The sleeves buttoned halfway between elbow and wrist, and the skirt hung in gentle folds around her calves.

"It looks even better than I thought it would." Sheila clapped her hands delightedly. "Now here's an apron to keep you clean until supper is served. May I try something a little different with your hair? I won't take long."

Jerusha didn't object as Sheila loosed her tight bun. "You have lovely hair. Why do you keep it pinned up so tightly?"

"Just to keep it out of the way, I guess." Jerusha tried to laugh, wondering why a different hairstyle should make her feel so uneasy.

"I'll show you how hair like yours should be worn, and it won't be in the way, I promise." She combed, twisted, and pinned. "There. You can feel what I've done, but touch it gently."

Jerusha reached exploring fingers to the back of her head. Her hair felt loose along the sides, yet it didn't fall into her face. It had been pulled back gently, then tucked into a soft roll. The looking glass on a nearby wall revealed the overall effect of softness.

"I can't believe this is me," Jerusha giggled. "I look almost pretty. Is that vain?"

Sheila hugged her. "Not at all. You look just as I've always thought you'd look if you let yourself be more a woman and less a preacher's sister. Too bad your army friend won't be here."

Still looking in the mirror, Jerusha saw herself blush. "He's not MY army friend. He's actually more David's friend than mine."

Sheila wisely said nothing. Feeling more defensive than ever, Jerusha hurried back out to the kitchen to check on the pie. Hopefully Lewis would come in before the roast overcooked. She had just decided to try to keep it warm on the back of the stove when she heard boots stamping on the porch. It sounded like someone had accompanied him.

"I invited this stray for supper." Lewis stopped as soon as he stepped inside, looking first at his wife in the rocking chair reading, then to his dressed-up sons, then at the fancy table, then at Jerusha. "Looks like you picked the right night, Keith." He moved to the side so both men could remove parkas and boots.

Jerusha felt intense heat from her neck to her hairline.

Sheila stood quickly and filled what could have been an awkward gap. "I'm glad you came, Corporal Sutherland. We're just celebrating my release from the sickroom. I hope you like parties."

"Yes, I do, ma'am. I hope you'll excuse my not being in dress uniform." His gaze strayed back to Jerusha, who stood as if glued in place.

Sheila laughed. "It's the company, not the clothes, that make the party. I've always thought men looked more handsome in work shirts than suits, anyway."

Jerusha willed her feet to move. Another china plate for the table, along with cutlery and a glass. *Continue slicing the roast. Make gravy. Potatoes and carrots in a bowl.* She had finished talking herself through the rest of the preparations by the time Lewis reappeared, washed and wearing a clean shirt. The boys chattered excitedly while Lewis asked Sheila quiet questions about her afternoon. Only Corporal Sutherland and Jerusha had nothing to say. She felt a strange happiness that he should see her at her feminine best, yet uncomfortable with her new appearance as well as the memory of last night's embrace. What must he think of her for allowing such contact? Her tears made the memory even more embarrassing. Every time she glanced at him, his gaze had not wavered from her.

Lewis asked a short blessing over the food, including a heartfelt thanks for his wife's recovery. When Sheila reached for the serving dishes to begin filling her sons' plates, he stopped her with a gentle reprimand. "No lifting, wife. Jerusha and I can help the boys." Glad for activity, Jerusha concentrated on mashing Bradley's potatoes and cutting his meat. Sheila plied the corporal with inquiries about his work. With his attention distracted, Jerusha felt her tension easing.

By the end of the meal, Sheila had begun to look weary. Lewis noticed immediately. "Boys, how would you like to help me put Mommy to bed? You can find your favorite books and we'll read her some stories." Excited chatter indicated his sons' approval. He looked to Jerusha. "You don't mind being left with dishes?"

"I'll be glad to help her," Keith cut in.

"But you did that last night!" Jerusha's protest came instinctively. She hoped he wouldn't leave right away, but she didn't want to be left alone with him again. Or did she?

"It's a biblical principle that a man's got to work if he wants to eat. I just managed to get to the eating before the working." He grinned, and Lewis nodded agreement.

Jerusha helped Sheila to her room while Lewis got the boys into their night clothes. She reached for the buttons on the back of her dress. "I'd better change out of this before I start cleaning up. I'd hate to ruin it."

Sheila touched her arm to stop her. "I think the corporal would like it better if you didn't."

An unfamiliar quiver of pleasure tugged at Jerusha even though she continued her protests. "That's not a good reason."

"Why not? It looks to me like he's falling in love with you."

Jerusha took a deep breath to steady her voice. "I don't think that's a possibility. Besides, I came to Dawson Creek to help David, not find a husband."

Sheila raised her dark eyebrows. "Who knows what could happen? Hand me my nightgown, please. If I'm not in bed when Lewis gets back, he probably won't let me have my bedtime story." Jerusha laughed at her friend's foolishness, then helped her get comfortable.

When she returned to the kitchen, the table had already

been cleared.

"I don't know what to do with this stuff." Keith gestured helplessly at the leftovers. "You ladies always make it look so easy, but when I tried to do it at home I could never find the right size dish."

Jerusha chuckled in spite of herself. "I'm glad there's something you're not good at."

He winked. "I guess I just need lessons."

She felt her face heat again and wished desperately she could get over her intense responses to him.

"I can see it's a good thing I came out tonight," he offered quietly.

For the first time during the evening, she looked him straight in the eyes. "Why?"

"I thought our conversation last night might have left you uncomfortable. You don't have to be embarrassed at letting me see the person you are inside, Jerusha. I think you're pretty special, and I'm honored you'd trust me with what you think."

She shrugged, wishing she could regain her previous detachment. Emotions didn't get embarrassing when she kept her distance.

"I mean it, Rushi."

His use of David's nickname and his hand on her shoulder unsettled her too much. She jerked away.

"Hey!" His voice dropped almost to a whisper. "What is it?"

She backed further from him. "I wish you wouldn't touch me." She could feel his gaze on her face, though she concentrated on pouring gravy into the dish of potatoes.

"Jerusha, please look at me." The pleading in his voice reached her more intimately than a physical touch. "Please don't feel upset over last night. It's not weakness to need comfort. You're dealing with a lot of pain, and I believe God invented hugs to get us through those hard times. I'm glad I was the one He chose to help you."

She couldn't believe she'd heard him correctly. It seemed like he always saw her at her weakest emotionally. Was it possible he didn't despise her for accepting his comfort so readily?

"Please come sit down." He pulled the chair away from the end of the table. When she perched on the edge of it, he straddled the bench to her left so he could face her. "I hadn't intended to tell you this, but I feel you need to know. You've become a very special person to me, Jerusha. Though I'm not free to develop the kind of emotional bond with you I'd like to, I want to be your friend. I'll never judge you for being honest with me, and I'll never criticize you for not being the kind of person you think you ought to be. You're precious to me, and to God, just the way you are. Will you let me be your friend?"

She searched his eyes for hints of mockery or disdain, but found only compassion that seemed to come from the most tender places in his soul. She nodded.

"Will you promise not to shut me out even when you don't like the way you feel?"

The warmth in his eyes wrapped her in a blanket of safety. Maybe she didn't have to be perfect to be loved. All at once, God's love as he'd described it seemed possible. She could respond to that hope only with honesty. "I'll try."

"Good girl." The grin that always brightened her day lit the kitchen. "Now let's see what we can do about these dishes."

thirteen

Sheila continued to gain strength daily. Within two weeks, Dr. Pierce and Lewis deemed her hardy enough to manage without Jerusha. Not surprisingly, Keith showed up to take Jerusha back to town. She tried to ignore the conspiratorial twinkle in Sheila's eyes while she gave final instructions. "Don't you dare try laundry on your own for at least another month. I'll come out on Saturdays to help with that. Leave major cleaning for then, too."

"Yes, ma'am." Sheila ducked her head in pretended submission.

"I'll stick close to the house to make sure she behaves." Lewis reassured Jerusha with his small smile.

Keith held her overnight bag while she fastened her boots and heavy coat. She turned to say goodbye to the boys, who had seated themselves on the stairs.

"Why are you leaving, Auntie 'Rusha?" Bradley arranged his features in his most pathetic look.

"'Cause she has to help the preacher. He's her brother, you know," Colin informed him wisely.

"Will you ever come back?"

Colin awaited the answer as expectantly as Bradley. Jerusha felt their sad gazes tug at her heart. "Come here, both of you." She knelt on the floor so she could wrap them both in a hug. "We love each other, right?" They nodded solemnly. "Then that means we're always together even when we can't see each other. I'll be thinking of you with loving thoughts, and you'll be thinking of me. Besides, your Mommy and Daddy will bring you to church on Sundays, and I'll come out often to make sure your Mommy isn't working too hard." Grins lit both faces, and two pairs of chubby arms wrapped themselves around her neck.

"Ok, boys, let Auntie 'Rusha go home now so she can come back sooner," Sheila encouraged.

Keith and Jerusha made the trip back to town in silence. David greeted her with an enthusiastic hug, then invited Keith to come in for coffee. "This is going to feel like a regular party after weeks of silence," he commented.

"Silence?" Jerusha raised her eyebrows disbelievingly. "What happened to the unending stream of 'Reverend, could you please...'"

"It's not the same as family." He gave her another rough hug, then held her away from him at arms' length. "You've changed, little sister."

Jerusha felt the blush creeping up her face. No reply came to mind. David filled coffee cups and the three sat down at the table. He looked intently into her eyes.

"Have you perchance found answers to the questions you were asking the night you left?"

She looked quickly at Keith, wondering what his reaction would be to her honesty. Nothing showed in his gaze but the gentle concern to which she'd grown accustomed. She sighed deeply. "I don't know."

"You look more peaceful."

She forced herself to look directly at David. "I feel like I'm barely touching the edge of something wonderful, but I can't quite find it."

The enthusiastic twinkle in David's eyes softened to

encouragement. "Do you know what you're looking for?"

Jerusha nodded. "God's love. Sheila and I even talked about it some. All of you know what it's like. It just doesn't make sense to me."

A pause ensued. Keith looked down at the table, his lips moving silently. Finally David spoke. "You're closer than you think you are, Rushi. I can see it in your eyes. Don't try to live up to whatever you think His love is. You don't have to chase God. If you really want what He has to offer, He'll catch up with you." After a few more minutes of silence, the conversation moved quietly onto other topics. Eventually, a knock at the back door interrupted.

"Silence?" Jerusha asked David teasingly.

He just shrugged. She noticed he hardly limped at all as he moved toward the door.

She looked back at Keith. "Thanks for the ride."

"I was glad to help." The side of his mouth twitched with a suppressed grin. "Besides, if I hadn't come, I might not have learned about the problem here at the parsonage."

"Problem?" She wondered what she'd missed.

"You heard the preacher say it gets too quiet around here. I guess I'll have to keep a close eye on you two."

A lovely lighthearted sensation inside made her smile, though she didn't offer any comment. Maisie called from the entry, "Jerusha? Are you really home?"

Jerusha hugged her other friend delightedly. She'd missed Maisie more than she'd realized. "I'm really here, ready and willing to take all that laundry off your hands."

Maisie laughed. "It's not been that bad. Your lemon-juice trick kept my hands from aging before their time, though I had to use vinegar. Besides, your brother has helped a lot, or wasn't I supposed to tell her that?" She grinned at David.

"Now the secret's out, I guess I'll have to keep helping. I've gained a whole new appreciation for your little enterprise, Rushi. Leaving already, Keith?"

The corporal zipped his jacket. "'Fraid so. The army seems to like to see me around on a regular basis. Would it be okay if I brought a few of the guys over tomorrow evening? We have a growing number of new believers who'd like some place to go other than the bars."

"Is that too soon for you?" David asked Jerusha.

Not if it means Keith will come, too, she thought silently. Aloud she only said, "I think that will be fine."

"How about if I bring snow ice cream?" Maisie offered.

"The guys and I will find some popcorn, and we can have a regular party. But we don't want you to make any special preparations for us." He looked directly at Jerusha, giving her the feeling she'd just been given an order from a superior officer. At her nod of acknowledgement, he opened the door. "Until tomorrow night, then."

Jerusha spent the rest of the afternoon with Maisie, catching up on town chatter while they sorted laundry, cleaned the house, and prepared supper.

"Ruth Pierce told Mrs. Barry and I the doctor's quite impressed with how you helped Sheila, especially the day she lost the baby." Maisie's eyes glowed with pride for her friend. "You should have seen David's face when I told him. You'd have thought someone just declared you queen."

Jerusha shrugged. "I just hope I never have to live through another night like that."

"How's Sheila doing? About losing the baby, I mean."

Jerusha's hands ceased their scrubbing on the floor as

she contemplated. "I don't understand it, but she's peaceful. She's even found something to be glad about."

Maisie said nothing, watching Jerusha closely.

"She said she might never have realized Lewis loves her for herself if she hadn't lost Davey."

"You sound confused."

Jerusha looked at her friend directly. "It's like what you and Keith and David keep telling me about God. You say He loves me, but I always feel like I have to be something special to be worthy of His love. I wish I could feel about God's love the way Sheila does about Lewis'."

"If we could be good enough on our own for God's love, it wouldn't be such a miracle, would it?"

"David said the same thing. I just can't feel like it's true."

"That's where trust comes in, Rushi. Feelings often tell us something different about God than what He tells us about Himself in the Bible. We have to choose whether we're going to believe our feelings or believe Him."

The glimmer of hope Jerusha had felt since talking with Keith grew brighter. She silently resolved to do more Scripture reading. Maybe she could find something to show her whether God was like her imaginings or like her friends' descriptions.

Ever sensitive to others' feelings, Maisie quietly changed the subject. "Did I tell you what Kevin Pierce said to Mrs. Barry last week? It seems he's been learning about family relationships. He knows Mr. and Mrs. McEvan are his grandparents because they're Ruth's parents, and Mr. and Mrs. Pierce are his grandparents because they're Dr. Pierce's parents. But he couldn't figure out why they call Mrs. Barry Granny B. He decided it's because Mrs. Barry doesn't have a husband. 'You have to have a Grandpa to be a Grandma,' he told her. 'But you're just as nice as if you were a Grandma instead of a Granny.'"

Jerusha laughed, thinking how much the comment resembled something Colin would say. "What does he think of having an aunt and an uncle younger than he is?"

"I think the family has tried to prevent him figuring out the details of his family relationships. It's confusing enough to the rest of us."

"Mrs. McEvan doesn't look old enough to be Ruth's mother."

Maisie laughed. "She's not. I guess that's another Dawson Creek story you haven't heard."

"This town is full of unusual stories." Jerusha wrung out her scrubbing rag for the last time. "Do our drains work yet?"

"They're saying sometime in the spring. Since we're finished with the kitchen, how about a cup of tea while I tell you about McEvans?"

"Sounds good." Jerusha threw the water out the back door as usual, vaguely aware she didn't feel nearly as bothered by useless drains as she had a couple of months ago.

"Would you like to try one of Mrs. Barry's dried apple muffins?" Maisie already had the tea water heating, cups and saucers on the table, and she was reaching for small plates for the muffins.

Jerusha revelled in having someone else provide refreshment. "Sounds tasty."

"Any of Mrs. Barry's cooking is marvelous. Can't you tell by my waistline?" Maisie giggled, unembarrassed by her roundness. "Anyway, about McEvans. Mrs. McEvan came to Dawson Creek in the early thirties to teach in one of the country schools which used to be all over around here. Ruth and Phillip McEvan were in her school, and she took quite a shine to them. Apparently, their mother and three of their siblings had drowned in a river crossing a year or so previously. Little Greg was just an infant when it happened. The kids fell in love with Ida, and their dad followed suit. Theo and Ruth married only a month after Rachel was born, so Ruth's two boys fit between Ida's three youngest in age."

"What an incredible story!" Jerusha wanted to say romantic, but the word felt strange even in her thoughts. "How does Mrs. Barry come into it?"

"Mrs. McEvan lived in the boardinghouse before she got married. Neither of them will say much about it, but I get the feeling the wedding had a lot to do with Mrs. Barry's matchmaking skills. I think the dear lady has someone picked out for every unmarried person in Dawson Creek." Maisie giggled again, a faint blush darkening her cheeks.

"I hope she's found someone other than Sylvia for my brother."

Maisie's eyes widened. "What brought that on?"

Jerusha shook her head. "It's just that Sylvia seems to have decided David's her latest conquest, and whatever Sylvia wants, Sylvia gets."

"Are you sure it's not just David's lack of interest that's attracting her?"

"I don't know whether he's uninterested or not." Jerusha felt the worry twisting her stomach again. She could think of nothing worse than having Sylvia Irvine as a sister-in-law. "I've never seen him give her anything but the same friendly interest he gives everyone."

"Isn't that a good sign?"

"Sylvia appears to see it as a personal challenge. She's

going to get him to fall in love with her if he doesn't watch it. I have no idea what she's been up to since I haven't been in town."

"Jerusha, don't you think your brother can take care of himself?" Maisie put a comforting hand on Jerusha's arm, her voice carrying no reproach.

"He's just so interested in people, I'm afraid he's going to get taken advantage of."

"He also loves God too much to fall in love with someone who doesn't love God, too."

Jerusha filled her teacup thoughtfully. Part of her evaluated David's ability to withstand Sylvia, while the other part wondered what Keith would think. Would he also avoid someone who didn't love God as he did?

The conversation replayed itself in Jerusha's mind during the next evening. So many young adults showed up, the gathering moved to the meeting room. Maisie's ice cream disappeared in short order, along with the snacks brought by various other girls. The soldiers brought popcorn, as promised.

"May we use your kitchen to make this stuff edible?" Keith asked Jerusha.

She extended her hand for the bag. "I can do it."

"I know you can, but I already promised this impromptu party won't make any extra work for you. Just show me where to find a large pan and some bowls." His eyes twinkled at her.

Recognizing the futility of argument, she did as he asked, then wandered back into the meeting room. Several games were already in progress, Maisie was playing the piano for a group of singers, and an intense discussion of military strategy was underway. David concentrated on a game of chess while Sylvia hovered nearby. She noticed Jerusha come in.

"Miss Porter, I'm so glad to see you. David's cup is empty, and I wouldn't have a clue where to find the coffee pot." She fluttered her eyelashes at David, who looked at Jerusha with an understanding smile. "If you have any cocoa on hand, I'd love a cup of hot chocolate," Sylvia continued. "I'd understand, though, if you haven't been able to afford any."

Jerusha snatched David's cup without replying. If she didn't leave the room quickly, her ungracious feelings would burst out of hiding.

Keith started to grin at her when she re-entered the kitchen, but his expression quickly changed. "You look ready to cry or kill."

Jerusha tried to laugh. "It's Sylvia again. She's too helpless to refill coffee cups herself, then announces she'll understand if we can't afford to give her a cup of hot chocolate."

A muscle along Keith's jawline twitched. Though he smiled, his eyes looked cold as the winter sky. "Good thing I had some cocoa on hand from Mom's last care package. How about if you let me take the drinks out, and I'll let you finish the popcorn?"

"You'll let me?" Jerusha felt like laughing, surprised at how his understanding turned her anger into more pleasant feelings.

Keith's eyes softened with her laughter. "Pretty high-handed, aren't I? Guess it comes from too long in the army."

By the time the guests finally left, Jerusha couldn't believe how she'd enjoyed the evening. Keith seemed always on hand to make her laugh or draw her into another game.

He and Maisie were the last to leave.

"This was a great idea, Rev," he said. "We should do it more often."

"I'll agree to anything as long as it includes Miss Clarke's ice cream," David replied.

Keith's eyes took on what Jerusha recognized as his teasing twinkle. "Which means I don't have to bring popcorn next time?"

"Not so fast. The popcorn fills people up so there's more ice cream left for me."

Maisie blushed and grinned. Jerusha noticed for the first time how pretty her friend looked, especially when her eyes glowed. A strange silence gripped the four briefly.

Keith cleared his throat. "Miss Clarke, may I escort you back to the boardinghouse?"

"Thank you. Mrs. Barry gets irritable when I come home alone."

Keith reached for her coat, but David beat him to it. "Thanks again for helping Jerusha yesterday, Miss Clarke." He settled the coat on her shoulders with an unfamiliar expression on his face.

A wink from Keith caught Jerusha's attention. "Was it my imagination or did you enjoy yourself tonight?"

Her smile felt like it came from the happiest part of her heart. "I did, thanks to you."

"I'm glad you didn't let our resident fly in the ointment spoil your evening." He patted her shoulder. "See you soon. Don't work yourself too hard, or I'll have to take your brother out behind the woodshed."

David's chuckle blended with Maisie's laugh. "You should know by now, Corporal, how hard it is to slow my sister down when she has the working bit between her teeth."

Keith grinned. "Take care of yourself, too, Rev."

Long after the cold blast of Keith and Maisie's departure had vanished, a strange quiet lay over the parsonage. David had quickly bid Jerusha good night and vanished up to his loft bedroom. She noticed his lamp still burning even after she'd finished dishes and straightened the meeting room. Though glad to be alone, she didn't feel sleepy yet. Maybe this would be a good time to rediscover her Bible, which had sat untouched on the shelf by David's desk since they'd moved to Dawson Creek. A small piece of paper protruded from the top edge. She opened carefully to the place marked, only to see handwriting on the marker.

Jerusha, I've been expecting you to turn to Scripture soon. Nothing anyone says about God can replace what He says about Himself. I John is a good place to start. I'm praying for you. Keith

fourteen

Lewis arrived shortly after breakfast on Saturday morning to take Jerusha out to the farm. Thankfully, he seemed content to ride in silence. She found her mind occupied with Keith, trying not to be disappointed he had not appeared this morning to give her a ride. *He's already told you he's not interested in romance*, she reminded herself. *Besides, he can't just leave his army duties whenever he wants. Even if he were romantically inclined, he'd want someone like Maisie who shares his faith.* This brought her thoughts around to the Scripture passages she'd been reading whenever she found time. She'd followed Keith's suggestion and discovered a wealth of hope in the little book of I John.

Once at the farm, she found herself too busy for any kind of thinking. Colin and Bradley were so excited to see her, they wanted to be wherever she was. That slowed her cleaning and laundry considerably, but their endless chatter made the routine tasks more enjoyable.

"Auntie 'Rusha, Daddy says we can get a puppy when spring comes," Colin informed her with bright eyes.

"What's spring?" Bradley asked.

"It's when the snow melts," Colin informed him disdainfully.

Bradley wasn't impressed. "I asked Auntie 'Rusha. What's spring, Auntie 'Rusha?"

She looked over at Sheila, who watched her sons' antics

with a grin. Sheila just shrugged her shoulders. Jerusha knew if she didn't handle the question just right, she'd have one or both boys highly displeased.

"Well, Colin's mostly right, Bradley, but there's more to spring than just melting snow. Spring is when the sunshine feels warm enough you don't need a coat to go outside. There's usually lots of mud, which little boys like but mommies don't."

"Do aunties like mud?" Bradley had developed a love for impossible questions.

Jerusha smiled at him. "This one doesn't."

"Why?" Colin's curiosity had been aroused.

"Because everything gets dirty, and I like clean." She continued scrubbing the floor around the cookstove.

"Mommy does, too." Colin's face showed his disgust. "She even wants us clean, so she scrubs our faces and makes us take baths."

Both Sheila and Jerusha laughed. "I think your daddy likes clean," Jerusha pointed out.

"But he works in the barn!" Bradley seemed to feel the two ideas were incompatible.

"What does he do first thing when he comes inside?"

"He kisses Mommy!" Now the boys giggled in unison.

Jerusha grinned at Sheila. "Then what?"

The two thought for a moment, then the disappointing light dawned. "He washes his face and hands," Bradley said.

Colin's mind had already jumped to a new conclusion. "Does that mean I have to like clean when I get big?"

"I wouldn't worry about it too much now," Jerusha reassured him, picking up the bucket to dump the dirty water outside.

"How is the town drainage system?" Sheila asked when Jerusha came back in, shivering from her coatless exposure to winter.

"Still as useless as ever." Again, she noticed her strange resignation rather than irritation.

"And running water?"

"We have a well and an indoor pump, so I don't notice. But Maisie says the water system's just as bad as the drainage. Apparently the army is predicting improvement in the spring." She moved pots of heating water around on the stove. "Colin, would you bring me your dirty clothes from upstairs?"

"I can do it, too," Bradley asserted.

"All right. That would be a big help."

Strutting importantly, the two scrambled for the stairs.

"Any errands for me?" Sheila's face took on an innocent expression.

"Not a chance," Jerusha said firmly. "Rest while you can."

She paused in her laundry to make some soup and biscuits for lunch. The work went more quickly after Lewis sent the boys upstairs for naps.

"A short sleep probably wouldn't hurt you, either," he told Sheila, brushing her cheek gently with his fingers.

She gave him the gentle smile that always left a hollow feeling in Jerusha's middle. "I'd rather visit with Jerusha."

He nodded and clumped back out to the barnyard.

"So tell me the news." Sheila turned her rocking chair to face Jerusha's laundry tubs.

"I'm sure I'm not the best source for news. I don't have much contact with people outside the church." Jerusha scrubbed at some food stains on the front of a small shirt.

"I know you're always busy, which is one reason why I'm so grateful you've come. What do you do, besides laundry, I mean?" Sheila's laughter made Jerusha smile.

"David always has a steady stream of visitors, so I try to keep lots of bread on hand, and other goodies when I have time. Meals, regular housekeeping, and I've been doing some reading lately." All at once, she wanted to tell Sheila what she might have found.

"Reading? Like what?"

"The book of I John."

Sheila waited so long to reply, Jerusha looked up to see what she might be thinking. A brilliant smile rewarded her. "I'm so glad! Is it making any sense?"

"Some. It talks about God's love as if it were a fact, just like the sun coming up in the morning."

"'In this was manifested the love of God toward us, because that God sent his only begotten Son into the world, that we might live through him,'" Sheila quoted softly. "Are you remembering what the next verse be saying?"

Jerusha nodded, turning the handle on the wringer while she pushed socks and shirts through to the rinse water. "It seemed so strange to me when I first read it, it stuck in my memory. 'Herein is love, not that we loved God, but that he loved us, and sent his Son to be the propitiation for our sins.' I had to ask David about the propitiation part."

"And?" Sheila's face was alight with interest.

"He said it has to do with turning away God's wrath by offering a gift. In other words, God was angry with man's sin, so He sent His Son Jesus to die and become the sacrifice that would turn His anger away."

Sheila's voice was hushed. "Sure, and that's a lot of love!"

"You'd think I wouldn't have any more questions,

wouldn't you?" Jerusha concentrated on scrubbing the dirt out of Lewis' work pants.

"Maybe. What are you thinking?"

Jerusha pushed a pair of pants through the wringer before replying. "The book of I John seems to be divided equally between reassurances of God's love and statements about how we'll act and feel if we know God's love. I no sooner feel hopeful about it than I read one of those verses that shows me how far away I am."

Sheila walked over to where Jerusha bent over the scrub board and placed an arm around her friend's shoulders. "Those verses aren't there to be telling you what you need to be in order to be loved by God. They are for telling us what we'll be like when we know God's love for ourselves. The first step is to be believing what He says about His love. Sure and the rest will come."

Jerusha smiled her thanks for the reassurance and kept scrubbing. It still sounded too easy, yet at the same time, impossibly difficult.

Sheila let her work in silence for several minutes, then asked another question. "Has your army friend been visiting lately?"

Jerusha felt her cheeks warm. "He brought a bunch of army guys over a few nights ago for a party. We had a lot of fun."

"Sure, and is this Jerusha Porter I hear talking about fun?" Sheila's voice sounded playfully scandalized, her Irish brogue thickening. "He's good for you, I'm thinking."

"He has been a good friend." Jerusha made the statement more for her own benefit than her friend's.

"Friend? Aye. He was feeling a way more than friendship the night I dressed you up, 'tis sure!"

Jerusha tried to ignore the hope fluttering through her. "I'm sure it wasn't, Sheila."

"And why must that be?" Sheila's voice was heavy with Irish disapproval.

"He told me he'd never ask any woman to marry an army man. Besides, I'm not the kind he'd love." She dropped wet clothes into the clothes basket with more force than necessary.

"Faith, girl, and why not?"

To her annoyance, tears stung her eyes. "He'll choose someone sweet and gentle, someone who sees God like he does. I didn't come out here to get married, anyway."

"Jerusha, you're for trying to make yourself good enough for him, just like you are for God. Love doesn't come with a measuring stick. It just comes, surprising you with the joy of it all. He is saying he wouldn't ask a woman to marry him, but I'm thinking he never counted on meeting a pretty little preacher's sister with a kinder heart than she knows and a true desire to know God."

Any hope generated by Sheila's encouragement dribbled away as weeks passed without any word from Keith. Though she didn't want to, Jerusha found herself thinking more frequently of the compassion in his kind, gray eyes, the infectious grin that made her want to laugh, even the way he looked shorn right after he'd visited the army barber for another brush cut for his blond hair. Maybe he got sent overseas as he'd feared. Perhaps he'd realized how incompatible their ideas of God were and asked for a transfer so he wouldn't have to explain. *That's not the kind of man he is,* her heart told her. *He'll be back.*

Her tension grew. Her Bible sat beside her bed, once

again neglected as she kept herself too busy to think. Mrs. Barry's boarders seemed to use more linen than ever, and countless guests consumed her baking as fast as she could make it. When she went to bed in the evenings, fragments of Scripture chased each other through her mind. She wondered if the God she was beginning to find would vanish, too. Even Saturdays at the farm seemed difficult. Such a Saturday brought her to the breaking point.

As usual, the boys had hung around her knees, asking questions, telling stories, and generally getting in the way while she worked. She'd just finished scrubbing the kitchen floor when Bradley came running over to show her a picture he'd drawn. He tripped over his own feet and grabbed the laundry tub to steady himself. The hose came loose from the tub, pouring filthy, soapy water all over.

She didn't see the apologetic little boy. She only felt the effects of sleepless nights and unrelenting tension increased by a messy job she didn't want to do. "I wish you would stay out of the way! Look at the mess you've made." She hated the sharpness in her voice as much as the tears sliding down her cheeks. Clamping her lips together, she concentrated on wiping up the water.

Bradley retreated to his mother's arms. Jerusha heard Sheila explaining that Auntie 'Rusha knew Bradley hadn't meant to make a mess, but that she was tired today. She hated herself for having taken out her frustrations on the small boy. Yet if she softened enough to apologize, she might start crying uncontrollably. The boys stayed clear of her work area for the rest of the afternoon. Thorny remorse prevented her from appreciating the peace. She made their favorite oatmeal cookies while preparing supper for the family, and hugged them both extra tight before she left.

Bradley's lower lip trembled. "I'm really sorry, Auntie 'Rusha."

She forced herself to smile. "I'm sorry, too, Bradley. I know it wasn't your fault."

"It wasn't your fault, either." He wrapped his chubby arms around her neck and squeezed again. "Are you coming back sometime?"

"I think Sheila ought to be able to help next week," Lewis offered. "Then after that, I'll help her so you can have your Saturdays back."

Jerusha felt no better. Back at the parsonage, she prepared and served David's supper in a fog of preoccupation. Having spent so much time in Sheila's kitchen where the drain worked, she unthinkingly dumped her dish water down the sink. Thirty minutes later, it still hadn't drained, and she burst into tears. "I hate this horrible place! I just want to go home!" She collapsed at the table and burst into tears.

"Rushi!" David hurried from his desk to her side. "What is it, sister? I thought you were becoming happy here."

"I was," she sniffed. "But lately, everything's going wrong."

"Like what?" He rubbed her neck in his familiar comforting gesture.

She related her experience with Bradley, and Lewis' comment about next week. "He didn't say it, but I feel like they don't want me around anymore."

"That's not true, Rushi," David replied calmly. "They were talking to me. Wednesday night about how much you've helped. They have been concerned that you've been working so hard lately, though, and asked me if I felt two more Saturdays would be too much. But that's not all.

You miss Keith, too, don't you?"

She wanted to deny any such emotional attachment, but the mention of his name made her sob even harder.

"Hey, Rushi, it's all right. He'll come back." David's gentle tone made the words more than glib assurance.

"What if he doesn't?"

"I can't answer that. Have you tried talking it over with our Heavenly Father?"

Jerusha shook her head, looking at her brother through her tears. "I'm still not sure how I feel about God."

David dried her cheeks with the backs of his fingers. "Maybe that's the heart of your struggle. You're trying to figure Him out, instead of simply letting Him love you."

"I've been trying to feel His love, but it doesn't work."

"Love and trust go together, Rushi. You can't have one without the other. You've been reading Scripture. You know He says He loves you. If you trust what He says, then you can simply accept His love as fact. Until you decide to trust His word, you'll continue trying to live up to an impossible dream of what you ought to be. I would think acceptance is much easier." He smiled gently. "May I pray with you?"

When she nodded, he grasped both her hands in his and bowed his head. "Father, You know we've both come to Dawson Creek because we felt You called us here. You also know how hard it's been for Jerusha to adjust. She's been searching for Your love, Father. I know You're just waiting for her to accept what You offer. I'm asking You tonight to show her how real You are and what Your love is really like. Give her peace, Father, and please protect Keith wherever he is. In Jesus' name, Amen."

To Jerusha's relief, he didn't release her hands immediately. His words and his prayer had rekindled the spark of hope she'd felt before Keith left. She felt if she didn't acknowledge it verbally she might lose it again. "God, it seems strange to call You Father since I've not really known what a father is like. But You've shown me in the Bible that Your love is real and that I don't need to do anything special to deserve it. I accept Your love, Father. Please teach me how to know You like David and Keith do. David says trust and love work together, so I'm telling You that I choose to trust You. Amen."

David squeezed her hands so hard they hurt. When she looked up at him, tears spilled from his eyes. "You don't know how long I've prayed for this, Rushi. Keith's got to come back just so he can find out how our prayers have been answered."

She didn't feel sure anything significant had taken place. No blinding flash had taken away her doubts. But she did agree with him about Keith's return. A strange spark of hope told her he would be back.

fifteen

Jerusha woke Sunday morning feeling more refreshed than she had in months. She expected to hear birds singing outside her window until she remembered it was only the first week of April. Though snow was beginning to melt, she'd been told spring didn't come to this country until late May. Why, then, did she feel so lighthearted? Slowly, last night's conversation and prayers returned to memory. It seemed incredible her simple prayer could have made such a difference. David wouldn't be ready for breakfast for awhile yet. Maybe another look at I John would explain things. She opened her Bible and read until the eighth verse of the second chapter. "...The darkness is past, and the true light now shineth." That exactly described her feelings—like someone had turned on a warm, wonderful light inside her.

This would be a perfect morning for David's favorite breakfast, dried apple coffee cake. While she worked, she hummed a tune from her days in Sunday school. "I am so glad that Jesus loves me, Jesus loves me, Jesus loves me. I am so glad that Jesus loves me. Jesus loves even me." Somehow it actually made sense this morning. Of course, she didn't have to live up to anything to receive God's love. If she could earn it, it wouldn't be Divine love. She still wasn't sure how a holy God could love an imperfect human such as herself, but somehow it didn't really matter anymore. He said He loved, and for Jerusha, His assurance had become enough. An unfamiliar delightful emotion bubbled in her—kind of like contentment, but with lots of happiness mixed in, though more than happiness. She remembered something Sheila had said. "Love just comes, surprising you with the joy of it all." Was this joy? Whatever its definition, Jerusha wanted to feel it forever.

Sheila had actually been talking about Keith, she recalled. The familiar wondering anxiety encroached again. Jerusha felt her elation withering. *But I promised God last night I'd trust. Maybe I should trust Keith, too.* It wasn't easy, overcoming a habit of worry developed over years, but the simple resolve to try lifted her spirits again.

When their congregation gathered for worship, Jerusha experienced more unfamiliar emotions. She no longer felt threatened by the people gathering in the meeting room. She saw on their faces a bit of the joy she'd been revelling in all morning. In fact, she wanted to hug each one of them, even the ones she had resented for not doing more to help David. When Maisie arrived, she couldn't help herself. She wrapped her friend in a joyous, strangling embrace.

When she could breathe again, Maisie laughed. "I don't believe I know you anymore, Miss Porter. What's happened to my favorite uptight Miss Minister's Sister?"

Jerusha grinned, suddenly embarrassed by her display, glad only a few folks had arrived yet. "Last night David and I prayed. I decided to quit trying to figure God out and simply accept His promise to love me."

"Oh, Rushi, I'm just delighted!" This time Jerusha received the bone-crushing hug.

"'Tis good news over here, I'm thinking." Sheila's familiar Irish lilt interrupted the girls' happy conversation.

"The best," Maisie assured her. "Jerusha discovered last night God's not her enemy."

Sheila hugged both her friends ecstatically. "No wonder your eyes be sparkling. Now if we can get your army friend back in town!"

Jerusha felt her cheeks warm, but her heart didn't droop. "It's okay if he doesn't."

"Sure, and he won't be able to stay away." Sheila winked, then joined her husband and sons who were already seated.

Maisie nudged Jerusha. "Look over there. I think a couple of little people want your attention."

Bradley and Colin were both waving as enthusiastically as they could without attracting a reprimand from their dad. Jerusha's eyes stung. She still felt badly for yesterday's scene, but it appeared both boys had already forgotten it. She smiled and waved back. Rather than sitting in her customary place by herself at the end of the first row, she joined Maisie and Mrs. Barry a little further back. To her delight, she found some of the hymns exactly expressed her emotions. When members of the congregation gave testimonies, she no longer felt like she was listening to meaningless prattle. And David's sermon! It seemed like he'd written it just for her, though she knew he wouldn't embarrass her that way.

His text was Romans 8:15-17. "For ye have not received the spirit of bondage again to fear; but ye have received the Spirit of adoption, whereby we cry, Abba Father. The Spirit itself beareth witness with our spirit, that we are the children of God; And if children, then heirs; heirs of God, and joint-heirs with Christ." He looked around at the congregation with joy lighting his eyes. "I've come to realize in recent weeks how often our perceptions of God stand between us and all He has to offer. We often get the idea that we have to earn His love. Yet He says here that He gives us His spirit, which causes us to come to Him like little children do to their daddies. Kevin, are you afraid of your daddy?"

Kevin Pierce turned bashful, simply shaking his head and snuggling closer to Dr. Pierce.

"How about you, Colin?"

"Only if I make Mommy work too hard, 'cause then I know I'll get spanked."

The congregation laughed, Sheila blushed, and David continued. "But after the spanking, you're not afraid anymore, are you?"

"Nope." The answer came emphatically.

"That's the kind of relationship God wants with us as His children," David explained. "There are times our sin gets between us and Him, but Jesus' death is the solution we need. His sacrifice so fully atones for our sins—past, present, and future—that God is able to write them off as if they didn't exist.

"But there's more. Verse 17 says we're joint-heirs with Jesus. That means everything He has is ours. Ephesians 2:14 says He is peace, so we have peace. Other scriptures tell us of His righteousness, so we are righteous. Now look at the last five verses of Romans 8. Paul makes an incredible list of circumstances and events that could, in our minds, keep us apart from this incredible love. Yet he ends the chapter by saying none of those things will be able to separate us from Him. We may choose to live like it isn't there, but our decision can't affect His reality. When we're ready to accept it, He's still waiting to bestow His wealth on us."

The remainder of the day continued in the same marvelous theme. Maisie and Mrs. Barry stayed for lunch, and for once, Jerusha simply enjoyed having company. A collection of young people showed up later in the afternoon. Without any sense of inadequacy, Jerusha offered them refreshments. She felt like she'd been miraculously released from a prison built from her own expectations.

She filled the coffee pot for what seemed like the hundredth time. How long would this joyous miracle last? The thought briefly clouded her mental landscape. Squaring her shoulders, she decided to handle it if and when it happened. For now, she'd enjoy the euphoria. While waiting for the coffee, she prepared popcorn. There were a few baked goodies left, and Mrs. Barry had given them a couple dozen of her muffins that could be cut in half to go around. After passing around the food, she refilled cups.

"You're handling this well, Rushi!" David commented quietly as she leaned over his shoulder to pour him more coffee.

A joking retort popped into her mind and slid out her mouth before she realized what she'd said. "And what would you do if I weren't around anymore?"

His eyes widened for a moment until he realized she was teasing, then he teased right back. "I'd just have to find a pretty girl and marry her."

Sylvia Irvine and a couple of soldiers arrived at that moment, increasing the comment's significance in Jerusha's mind. Her better sense told her David wouldn't even consider falling in love with Sylvia, but the old obsession didn't die easily. She feared Sylvia more than any of the other girls, perhaps because the banker's daughter had a way of making Jerusha feel like a mere servant girl in spite of her honeyed words. Jerusha stayed by the stove, watching the crowded sitting room. Sylvia had taken up her customary position as close to David as possible. David smiled at her, and she fluttered her eyelashes at him. He started visiting with her, so she beckoned one of the soldiers into the conversation so she could flirt with both men at once. Just when Jerusha thought she could stand no more, David's sermon came back to her. "No circumstance or event can keep us apart from God's love." *Not even Sylvia?* she asked herself. From somewhere deep inside she felt reassured. Not even Sylvia could touch the deep joy she'd found.

To Jerusha's amazement, the joy continued. One of the hotels asked her to fill in for a week for their laundry lady who had sprained her wrist. While David and Maisie helped as much as they could, Jerusha still wondered if there would be enough hours in each day. Yet, the work got done. She even had time in the evenings for Scripture reading with David, a treat she anticipated throughout the day. His sermon from Romans 8 had drawn her from I John to Romans. In the mornings, she read by herself and in the evenings discussed with David what she'd read. She felt an unquenchable thirst to know more. Her awareness of Divine love still felt tenuous. Maybe finding out more about God would strengthen her hold on His reality.

David exuded more enthusiasm than usual. Members of their congregation were beginning to invite others to the services. Both Sunday and Wednesday services had filled the meeting room almost to capacity last week. The increased congregation meant more visitors to the parsonage and more demands on David's time, but Jerusha no longer battled resentment. She hoped everyone who came would encounter the same God she'd found.

One of their rare evenings alone made Jerusha wonder if her newly ordered world had begun to unravel. David asked a quiet question from where he sat at the table while she washed supper dishes. "What would you think of my getting married, Rushi?"

Images of Sylvia moving into the parsonage filled Jerusha's mind. Just as quickly, she knew it wouldn't work, and she tried to envision a steady stream of visitors in and out of a fancy house like Irvines'. That didn't seem feasible, either. "It would depend on who you wanted to marry." She kept her eyes on the dishes.

A long pause followed. Then, so quietly she almost didn't hear him, David replied. "I'd like to ask Maisie Clarke to become my wife."

Jerusha whirled around in surprise, the soapy plate she held slipping to the floor. "Maisie?" she squeaked.

"I'm not trying to take your friend away, I promise. In fact, I thought it might be easier for the three of us to live together since you two are so close." An unfamiliar blush tinged his face.

The blush calmed Jerusha's shock, pushing her to tease him a bit. "You mean you decided you wanted to marry her just so your wife and your sister would get along?"

He reddened further, even while his twinkling eyes acknowledged her humor. "No. I love her more than I thought possible. I just don't want you to feel pushed out of either of our lives if she says yes."

"You haven't asked her yet?"

He shook his head. "I wanted your opinion first. I hoped it would give me the courage to put my feelings into words."

David lacked courage? The thought didn't fit in Jerusha's mind. "Does she have any clue how you feel?"

"I hope so." He traced circles on the tabletop. "We spent a lot of time together while you were out at Murrays' and

I was helping her and Mrs. Barry with laundry. I discovered her tender heart, her marvelous sense of humor, and most of all, her passionate love for God. It wasn't until after you came back, though, that I realized I love her. I've gone over to the boardinghouse several Saturdays while you've been out at the farm, and I think she returns my feelings. But I won't know until I ask her straight out and the mere thought gives me the trembles."

The sight of her brother trembling at the thought of proposing to her best friend almost gave Jerusha the giggles. She tried to recall anything Maisie had said or done that she might be able to use to encourage him. But it seemed she'd been so involved in her own turmoil, she'd missed any hint of this developing romance. "I wish I knew what to say, David. I was so afraid you were falling for Sylvia Irvine I never even thought of you being interested in anyone else."

His head snapped up. "Sylvia Irvine? Why would I fall for her?"

Now Jerusha felt embarrassed. "Because she tries so hard to get your attention. Besides, she always looks so beautiful and acts like such a lady."

"Fine clothes are well and good in their place, but they can't cover a person's heart." He walked over to put his hands on Jerusha's shoulders. "Even if Maisie turns me down, I want you to know I'll never consider any woman who isn't kind to my sister. I won't abandon you, Rushi."

She blinked away unwanted tears, wrapping her arms around her brother in the first hug she'd initiated toward him in years. "Thanks, David. You don't know how much that means to me." She pulled back to look into his eyes with a grin. "But for tonight, I think you have more important business than settling my feminine fears. Go get your preachin' suit on, or should I call it your courtin' suit, and get out of here."

He didn't return for several hours, which Jerusha took as a good sign. Intuition told her Maisie would accept his proposal. But where would they put a third person in this tiny cabin? Would she and Maisie be able to work together harmoniously? Maybe she should consider taking Maisie's place at Mrs. Barry's. Would she ever have the opportunity to make the decision Maisie was making? If not, would she live as an old maid aunt with David and his wife forever? What if his wife got tired of having her around all the time? *Nothing "shall be able to separate us from the love of God..."* The fragment of Scripture calmed her tumbling thoughts, though she wished she could answer all the questions. She finally gave up waiting for David and went to bed. As she fell asleep, the verse played through her mind like a lullaby. *Nothing "shall be able to separate us from the love of God..."*

David's glowing face the next morning told her Maisie's answer, though he seemed to feel an explanation was needed. "She said yes, Rushi! I can't believe how blessed I am. Mrs. Barry wants to throw an engagement party here tonight during the youth meeting, and she said to tell you she'll bring everything. I stayed so late because we just had so much to talk about." He chattered on while Jerusha served breakfast.

She bent over his chair to hug him, delighted for his happiness. "I'm excited for you, David. Now, will you please hush and eat?"

He grinned self-consciously and consumed three bowls of oatmeal, then decided he needed to take a walk "to clear his mind." Jerusha giggled to herself as the door shut behind him, relieved he was getting out of the house. She wanted to give it a top-to-bottom cleaning. In his present mood, he'd only get in the way. She worked steadily, pondering life's changes. Like the contentment that now filled her days instead of the resentment of not so long ago. What a miracle her simple prayer had brought about! Yet another simple prayer remained unanswered. As she was learning to do each time she thought of Keith, she asked again for Divine protection for him.

Hunger rumblings brought her work to a halt about midafternoon. When she realized the time, she wondered briefly why David hadn't returned. *He probably "wandered" by the boardinghouse and stayed for lunch*, she told herself with a grin. Tonight would be a good time to serve a special meal. After putting her lunch dishes by the sink, she rummaged through the box of wrapped meat that sat frozen in the coldest corner of the porch. Gratefully remembering the members of their congregation who kept them supplied with meat from their own herds, flocks, and hunting expeditions, she found a chicken. It had been a long time since she'd made fried chicken, David's favorite dinner. She still had enough potatoes to make mashed potatoes, all creamy and fluffy like he liked them. Some canned corn would also be nice, and how would dried apples work in apple pie? Feeling reckless, she decided to try it.

David finally returned around 4:00. "Sorry I was gone so long, Rushi. I just stopped for a moment at the boardinghouse, and Mrs. Barry invited me for lunch. Then I got to helping Maisie with some cleaning, and I forgot the time."

Jerusha just laughed at him. "I'm not expecting your brain to be in working order. Did you happen to notice whether the ladies mentioned what time they'll be arriving tonight?"

He looked faintly embarrassed. "I invited them for supper. I hope you don't mind."

She could only laugh again. "Not at all. I just hope you guys haven't planned a long engagement. Six months of this could get stressful."

"June 8," he announced, climbing the ladder to the loft.

It took Jerusha a moment to realize he'd told her the wedding date. Supper was an hilariously happy affair. None of the four could stop smiling, though Mrs. Barry and Jerusha found their conversation more coherent than David and Maisie's. Maisie tried to include the others, but her eyes kept looking back in David's direction. His gaze never wavered from her face. Mrs. Barry shooed them into the sitting room after dessert. "Neither of you is good for anything tonight, so just go somewhere out of the way. Now, dear," she addressed Jerusha. "I think I can find my way around in here if you'd like to go change into something festive."

Jerusha started to protest that she had nothing, then remembered the burgundy dress Sheila had given her. "Thanks. I'll be right back."

"There's no need to rush." Mrs. Barry's smile looked purely maternal.

Jerusha intended to slip into the dress quickly, tie on an apron, and return to the kitchen. Instead she found herself sitting beside the dress on the bed, remembering the first time she'd worn it, the way Keith's gaze had followed her as David's did Maisie. Whether or not he loved her, he'd promised her his friendship. She sent up another fervent prayer for his return, at least so she could tell him how she'd changed. Once she had donned the dress, she realized her hair wouldn't do at all. She combed it out carefully, then tried to arrange it as Sheila had. The small mirror on her wall twenty minutes later indicated the time had been well spent.

"What a beauty!" David whistled when she came back to the kitchen.

She hid her feelings behind a laugh. "I didn't think you'd even notice!"

"Of course I notice. My fianc—" he choked on the word with a silly grin, then tried again. "My fiancée will be the most beautiful woman here tonight, and my sister will be a very close second."

Maisie beamed. "You do look gorgeous, Jerusha."

Guests started arriving less than half an hour later. Mrs. Barry had outdone herself with a lavish spread of goodies.

"Where did you get the sugar for all this?" Jerusha asked, thinking of how often she'd tried unsuccessfully to buy the sweetener. The local stores seemed unable to keep it in stock for more than a couple of days. It was just one more challenge that accompanied living in an over-crowded town.

"I have my ways." The older lady's eyes twinkled. "Some of the squares are made with honey from my son's farm."

Though David had planned to keep his announcement for later in the evening, his and Maisie's faces gave the secret away. The word spread as quickly as people shed their coats and boots. Sylvia's eyes looked like little bits of blue granite when one of the soldiers gave her the news, though she kept a smile firmly in place. "Maybe you should offer Miss Porter your job at the boardinghouse so you can have the preacher all to yourself," she suggested to Maisie with a shrill titter.

"Never!" Maisie declared, with a harsher expression on her face than Jerusha had ever seen. "I wouldn't let her leave us for anything other than a husband of her own."

Jerusha looked quickly to David, who winked and smiled. *He really did mean what he said about marrying someone who would love me, too.* The thought restored her earlier sense of well-being. Though the details might not be easy, she could feel enough love among the three of them to overcome the challenges.

Mrs. Barry had even brought extra glasses, which she now handed around. "I thought lemonade would be a nice treat for tonight. Please don't take a drink until everyone gets a glass." She continued passing the glasses around, taking the final glass for herself. "The world uses alcoholic beverages to drink a toast for special occasions. I'd like to propose a blessing to which you can agree by raising your glass and saying 'Amen.' David and Maisie, we all wish for you God's best as you build your home and do the work He gives you. We pray He'll give you many years together, each marked with a love more mature than the year before."

Jerusha echoed "Amen" with the others, feeling a tightness in her throat as she looked at her brother and her friend, their eyes filled with love for each other. Someone cracked a joke she didn't quite hear, and the ensuing laughter almost drowned out a knock at the door.

sixteen

A cold blast just before she reached the entry told Jerusha their visitor hadn't waited to be invited inside. Her eyes had barely registered the delightfully familiar grin and gray eyes under a khaki hat before she was engulfed in a cold bear hug. "I've missed you!" a welcome gruff voice declared.

Her arms wrapped themselves around him instinctively. "Keith! Welcome back!"

He pushed her away to study her face, then smiled into her eyes. "You look like you're doing wonderfully well. What's the noise about?"

Jerusha laughed joyously. "David's engaged to Maisie Clarke. Mrs. Barry threw a party for them tonight." Slivers of pain dimmed the happy twinkle in his eyes. She looked for words to ease his hurt, hoping she hadn't caused it. "He'll be so glad you managed to be here!"

Keith dropped his gaze for a few moments, then his eyes cleared when he looked at her again. "I'm glad, too. Let's go help them celebrate."

The merrymaking continued, taking on the joyous sparkle Jerusha remembered from youth gatherings right after she returned from the farm. It was well after ten when the last guest departed.

Keith slapped David's back. "There's no need to ask if you're sure about this, Rev. That goofy grin tells it all."

With an arm around her shoulders, David hugged Maisie

closer to him. "You know what Proverbs says, Keith. 'He who finds a wife finds a good thing....'"

"Yeah, I know. I'm glad for you both." He grinned at them while picking up cups to take to the kitchen.

Jerusha wondered if anyone else heard the strangling sound in his voice. She wanted to wrap her arms around him and take his pain into her own heart, even though she had no idea what weighed on him so intensely. She absent-mindedly wiped dishes as Mrs. Barry washed.

"There. We have your kitchen back in order," Mrs. Barry announced. "Amazingly enough, they didn't eat all the cake or apple muffins, so I'm leaving them for you and David, though I get the feeling I'll be cooking for him more often than you will." She fixed Jerusha with a direct look. "Promise me if you get to feeling abandoned or left out, you'll invite yourself to the boardinghouse for dinner."

Jerusha's eyes stung from unexpected tears. The affection offered by this perceptive lady seemed too good to be true. She nodded. "I promise."

"I'll be doing what I can to keep her from getting too lonely, Mrs. Barry." Keith's hands came to rest lightly on Jerusha's shoulders.

Mrs. Barry's eyes twinkled with understanding and something else Jerusha couldn't identify. "I'll hold you to that, soldier."

"I recognize that tone of voice, Mrs. B.," Maisie called. "Are you matchmaking again?"

"Of course not," the older lady declared indignantly while Jerusha felt her cheeks warm and Keith's hands tremble on her shoulders. "I'm just making sure Jerusha doesn't feel forgotten while you and the reverend wander around with your heads in the clouds. Reverend, I think I'm ready to go. I'd appreciate it if you'd escort us home, though you're welcome to use my parlor as long as you like."

Now Maisie's cheeks turned pink. "She means she wants to get home, but she doesn't want us to feel in a hurry to say good night. Subtle as a tank, isn't she?"

"Mrs. Barry, you're a jewel." David hugged her shoulders. "Of course I don't mind taking you home, though I might tie up your parlor for quite awhile."

Maisie swatted his arm. "You'd better. We still have a lot of planning to do."

The three teased each other all the way out the door. Jerusha could hear David's laugh echoing from outside.

"I've always been afraid marriage would take him away from me," she mused aloud. "But he's so happy right now, I don't care anymore."

Keith leaned against the counter, facing her. "Have they talked with you yet about your plans?"

She laughed. "They're not at the practical stage yet. However, they've both told me how much they want me to continue living here after they're married."

Keith looked around the cabin. "This little place could get crowded."

"We'll manage," she reassured him with a smile.

He looked at her intently. "Rushi, what's happened to you?"

"What do you mean?"

He took her hand and drew her toward the sitting room, where he pulled her onto the padded bench against the wall. "Before I left, you would have been in a panic about David's getting married, with a thousand questions about the future." He chuckled softly. "I kind of think you might even have been talking about hopping the first train back to

Winnipeg. Instead, I find you smiling and at peace. What's happened?

She didn't know how to begin. His absence had been one of the most insistent issues pushing her toward surrender, but she couldn't tell him so. "Do you want just an overview, or all the details?"

He slouched back against the wall, his legs out in front of him, and gave her the incredible grin that had brightened her memories. "I've got the rest of the night if you need it. All the details, please."

She told him about continuing to help at the Murrays and the additional laundry work load she'd picked up. "You weren't around anymore, and I kept thinking you'd been sent somewhere dangerous. When I tried to sleep, all my questions and fears and wonderings about God and life in general muddled my brain, so I'd just lay there staring at the darkness. I'd been reading in my Bible, and everything I read contradicted so many things I thought were important. Finally, a couple of Saturdays ago, I lost my temper at Bradley over something he didn't mean to do. I realized I had to change something before I fell apart completely. That night David and I talked about it and he helped me see my problem was in trying to figure God out rather than simply taking Him at His word. He prayed for me and I told God how I felt. It felt like somebody had finally turned on a light after I'd been stumbling around for ages in darkness. Every time I start to feel overwhelmed, I remind myself God loves me and choose to trust Him. It's worked every time so far."

"And it won't ever stop working. That's the basics of faith—knowing who God is and choosing to believe. Peace looks good on you, Rushi." He shifted on the bench, but retained his gentle grip on her hand. His smile held something that made Jerusha's heart pound and left a trembly feeling in her middle. "Your discovery is an answer to my most heartfelt prayers. It also makes what I want to tell you and ask you easier. Though it's what I came for tonight, I don't think I could go through with it if I didn't know you'll have Divine love supporting you."

Her throat constricted. Was this good-bye? She forced herself to take a deep breath and hear him out.

He seemed to sense her apprehension and reached for her other hand. His felt chilly. "I have to apologize again for leaving without telling you. Unfortunately, that's the way the army works—everything happens right now unless, of course, you need it right now. In that case you have to wait at least a month."

He smiled tightly at his own joke. After a heavy sigh and a long pause, he continued. "Though nobody's supposed to know this, we're in a series of false maneuvers designed to confuse the Japanese. The end of the maneuvers for all of us will be Alaska, and from there, probably overseas."

Jerusha couldn't stop the whimper of surprise, which she tried to cover with a smile. "When do you leave?"

"Day after tomorrow." He didn't look at her now. He still held her hands, stroking her fingers with his thumb. "Jerusha, I think I fell in love with you that night you almost fainted by David's bed. I've alternately analyzed and ignored my feelings because I didn't want you to be hurt further by what may or may not happen to me. I thought we could just be friends, allowing me the pleasure of your company without any painful emotional ties." He lifted his gaze to her eyes, revealing infinite tenderness shadowed by an agony for the future. "Rushi, you've become part of my heart. The joy in your eyes makes me wonder if I can ever love you any more than I do right now. Much as I'd like to do differently, I won't ask for a commitment right now. I'd have to be some kind of cad to ask you to love me, then disappear, maybe forever. However, if I'm still alive when this horrible war is over, may I come looking for you?"

A million thoughts and images went through Jerusha's mind while she looked into Keith's eyes, drinking in the unfathomable love she saw there. This seemed too sudden, too intense. How could she live up to his kind of faith? He could get killed, and how would she ever know? It didn't make sense. It didn't even feel proper. She could get her heart broken, feeling like this. Yet the certainty remained—she loved him as he loved her. "Please do. I'll make sure I'm not hard to find."

The pain in his eyes receded behind a joyous glow. "You don't know what it means to me, Rushi." He hugged her tenderly, and she knew she'd be forever content in that embrace. "I wish I knew for sure whether I'll come back. I'll send your address to Mom tomorrow, so you'll be notified if—"

She pulled back to put a hand on his lips. "Don't say anymore, Keith. You've told me we can trust God to take care of even the smallest details. He won't make a mistake on something this important."

Moisture filled his eyes, though only a single tear escaped. "You really believe, it, don't you?"

"Yes," she whispered, still clinging to his gentle gaze.

"Don't ever give it up, no matter what you hear." He tenderly touched her lips with his.

She wrapped her arms around his neck when he kissed

her a second time, wishing she could hold him there, yet knowing the God she'd recently discovered could care for him far better than she.

"Another kiss like that and I won't be able to leave," he whispered, brushing his fingers across her lips.

She lay her head on his chest, soaking up the security of his presence. Would she miss him more or less now that they'd put their feelings into words?

His fingers explored the edges of her hairline. "I like what you did with your hair tonight."

"Sheila showed me how."

His chuckle vibrated against her cheek. "I remember that evening. You looked both stunningly beautiful and absolutely terrified."

"Hmmm." She remembered all too well.

"Ever since then I've wanted to see your hair down," he whispered. "Would you mind taking your pins out?"

Without lifting her head, she released the style she'd worked on for about half an hour to get just right. He ran his fingers through the locks as they tumbled down her back. "Have you ever cut your hair?"

"No. Mom and Aunt Vivienne always said short hair on women is a sign of rebellion."

"What do you think?" His fingers maintained a caressing rhythm, smoothing out tangles.

"I don't know. This is the way it's always been, so I don't think much about it. Maisie has short hair, and David doesn't seem to mind."

"I hope you never cut it."

"Why?"

He tipped her chin up so he could look into her eyes. "Because I think it's beautiful." He planted another kiss on her lips.

"Is it vain of me to be so pleased to hear you say so?"

His grin reached into the places of her heart where insecurity still lingered. "Not at all, my proper little worry wart. And to prove it, I'll tell you again. I think you're beautiful. Not just your hair, but all the way through. You're a lovely person both inside and out, Miss Porter." A kiss confirmed his words.

Gentle silence enveloped them. She would have thought his impending departure would make them want to discuss everything they could think of. Instead, she felt like too many words would mar the bliss of these last moments together.

David returned home. Though a smile lit his eyes when he saw them, he said nothing. He rummaged in the kitchen for a few moments, then returned carrying a small kerosene lamp he'd lit. Still without a word, he placed the lamp on the crate they used as an end table, turned out the electric light, and climbed up to his room.

"Hmm. Your brother's a clever man," Keith murmured with a hint of a chuckle in his voice.

Jerusha had her answer ready. "Of course he is. He told me a long time ago I needed to let you be my friend."

He looked down into her face again, the flickering kerosene flame reflecting in his eyes. "Did he really?"

"Um hmm." She laid an arm across his broad chest in a half hug. "He was right."

He embraced her closer, and the comforting silence enfolded them again. She felt him lay his cheek against the top of her head. At long last he stirred, and lifted his watch to the light. "I hate to do this, Rushi," he whispered, "but I'm on duty in a couple of hours."

Setting a light kiss on her lips, he sifted his fingers through her hair one more time. "I wish I had words to tell you what it means to know you'll be waiting and praying for me." Pulling her up to stand beside him, he looked into her eyes for several long moments.

She cupped his face in her hands. "God will keep us both."

He nodded and backed toward the door, zipping his parka without breaking eye contact. "I'll be back as soon as I can."

seventeen

Keith stopped by once more before he left. "Here's something I ordered for you, and it's finally arrived." He offered a large, paper-wrapped package.

Jerusha fumbled with the string, finally unveiling a dozen lemons. Tears sprang to her eyes. "How did you get so many?"

"Connections." His grin didn't stretch beyond his mouth. "I wanted to make sure you'd have enough until I can get you some more."

She heard the unspoken promise. "I'll think of you every time I do laundry."

"Only then?" A glimmer of his humor peeked from his shadowed eyes.

"Always."

He kissed her goodbye, an intense, lingering kiss despite David and Maisie sitting at the table. Lifting his hat in salute, he disappeared down the street. She stood at the window, watching until she couldn't see him anymore.

Jerusha turned away from the window to find David and Maisie watching her. David wiggled his eyebrows dramatically. "I'm glad you two have finally made it past the Corporal and Miss Porter stage. When's he coming back?"

"He doesn't know." Her world suddenly felt empty except for cold crystals of fear. She sank into a chair beside Maisie.

"Does he know where he's going?" her friend asked quietly.

"No."

David nodded with sudden understanding and reached for her hand. "'He shall give his angels charge over thee, to keep thee in all thy ways,'" he quoted softly. "'A thousand shall fall at thy side, and ten thousand at thy right hand; but it shall not come nigh thee.'"

She recognized the words as Scripture and felt like he'd offered her a place beside a warm fire on a cold day. "Where are those verses from?"

"Psalm 91. The whole thing is good for times like this."

As Peace River Country winter slowly gave way to spring, Jerusha read the Psalm every morning and every evening. For the first few weeks, it seemed like a thousand times a day, she had to choose to trust instead of worry. Gradually, fear retreated, replaced by confidence in God's love.

Warm weather finally arrived, bringing with it a new water and sewer system for Dawson Creek. One Saturday, three weeks before David and Maisie's wedding, a delegation of men arrived at the parsonage. Jerusha invited them in for coffee and fresh bread.

"Thanks, Miss Porter, but we just have to speak briefly with the reverend." Big, gray-haired Timothy McEvan seemed to be acting as the group's spokesman.

David shook hands all around. "Do we need to go somewhere private?"

"No, no. It's this way, Rev. With you and Miss Clarke gettin' married, we figgered you might need more room in this here cabin. We hope you don't mind, but we've got a bit of a plan to show you. Greg, show Preacher what you've got."

The younger man spread a piece of paper on the table. "I

heard Ma and Ruth and Mrs. Barry talkin' one night, and this idea came to mind. We can add another couple of rooms along the back wall, to give Miss Porter a new bedroom and her own sittin' room area, kinda. What is now Miss Porter's room could be expanded to be big enough for two by moving the wall into what is now the porch. We can also expand your present sitting room into the porch so you have more room for youth meetin's and such, and then build a new porch big enough for clotheslines for Miss Porter in the winter."

"That's a lot of work and lumber, Greg." David stated the fact without condemnation for the young man's idea.

"Which is why we're here, Rev." Mr. McEvan took over again. "There's another five or six men plannin' to get here soon, and with all of us workin', we can have everything done before nightfall." He held up a hand to stop David's objection. "We figure all of us together can carry the cost of the lumber. That and the day's work will be the church's wedding gift to you and Miss Clarke, though I know the womenfolk will add their own gifts later on."

David looked as overwhelmed as Jerusha felt. "How does it sound to you, Jerusha?"

She could only nod, amazed so many people wanted to put out the effort to make them more comfortable. "I'll go get my things out of the way."

True to their word, the men finished in a single day. They declined Jerusha's offer of supper, hurrying home to their families. David went to get Maisie so the three could explore their new home together. The new enclosed porch area ran the length of the parsonage now, with shelves on the north side and a trap door to a shallow area insulated with sawdust which would keep vegetables cool in the summer and meat frozen in the winter. Clotheslines had been strung across that end of the porch, as well. Shelves at the opposite end could hold boots and other items for storage. Pegs for coats extended from the doorway to the clotheslines. Only a small entry area was left from the old porch. A doorway to the right led to Jerusha's new quarters, which included both a bedroom and a small sitting room as promised. To the left of the entry, a doorway led directly into the enlarged main sitting room. The men had even created an alcove at one end for David's study area, complete with shelves. Jerusha's old room had also been enlarged to give David and Maisie plenty of bedroom space. Sturdy stairs beside the bedroom now replaced the old ladder up to the loft.

"They did this all today?" Maisie asked in amazement.

"Close to two dozen men worked on it," David explained.

"Still, it's incredible. They did it for free?"

"Welcome to a pastor's family, sweetheart." David put his arms around her. "Just when you begin to think no one notices you're living on a shoestring, the congregation will do something like this. They don't have much money, but they do have lots of heart."

Jerusha stuffed more wood into the cookstove. The changes in her house made the changes in her family more real. Though she and Maisie were close friends, what would it be like sharing cooking responsibilities and cleaning duties? How would Maisie want to decorate what would become her home?

Maisie became Mrs. David Porter on one of the sunniest days Dawson Creek had seen yet that spring. Granted, it was also one of the muddiest, but no one noticed. Army Chaplain Tom Silverman had agreed to perform the ceremony. Mrs. Barry took charge of preparing refreshments for afterward, and it seemed every lady in the congregation had joined in the effort. Gifts poured in, even from people not connected with the church. Canned goods, linens, and dishes quickly filled the remaining shelf space in the parsonage. Uncle Cam and Aunt Vivienne sent two train tickets for a wedding trip back to Winnipeg, along with the promise of a similar holiday for Jerusha later in the year.

But as the summer unfolded, Jerusha found herself not inclined to leave town. Dawson Creek had become home. Maisie did make changes in the parsonage, but Jerusha felt they made the expanded cabin friendlier and brighter. Since Maisie loved to cook, something Jerusha had only done of necessity, Jerusha rarely had to prepare a meal. This left her with more free time than she could ever remember having, even after her laundry duties were done. She visited more often with the Murrays, and became better acquainted with Mrs. Barry and Mrs. Pierce. And she wrote letters.

A brief note had arrived from Keith just before the wedding. She sent her reply to the address he'd indicated, but had heard nothing since. She kept writing, hoping her letters would catch up with him someday.

Her first letter from Mrs. Sutherland arrived while David and Maisie were on their wedding trip. When she'd first glimpsed the Colorado postmark, she'd been sure the letter contained the news she feared. It turned out to be just a letter of introduction. "Keith has written so much about you," it read, "that I almost feel like I know you. I think we could be great friends if we knew one another better. Since travel is out of the question, would you mind writing to me? I hear so rarely from Keith. It would be like a faint contact with him if I could hear from you." Jerusha wrote back immediately, apprehensive about writing to someone she didn't know, but eager to learn about Keith's family. From there the correspondence flourished.

Autumn replaced summer sooner than Jerusha thought it should. Winter came on even more quickly. Christmas held more excitement for her than ever before. Its story now told of Someone she was learning to know personally, rather than just being a religious story. Miraculously, a small package arrived from Keith—a lovely green, soft woolen scarf with matching gloves. Mrs. Sutherland sent several yards of royal blue silky fabric with a note. *"I've had this piece for several years, but my husband isn't fond of the color. I would be delighted if it suits you."*

Sheila squealed with glee when she saw it. "This will look stunning. May I make it up for you? I know exactly what to do with it."

Jerusha described the new dress in as much detail as she could for Keith. *"It has long sleeves, with cuffs which reach almost to my elbows. It also has a high collar with lace on it and on the cuffs. The skirt is long and full. It's absolutely luxurious to wear."* She went on to tell him as much Dawson Creek news as she could remember, including descriptions of new buildings that had been built. *"You're not going to recognize this place when you get back. It's ever so slowly turning from a grubby army village into an honest-to-goodness town. Some areas are particularly pretty during the summer. They'd be ideal for long evening walks.*

"The scarf and gloves you sent me are just as beautiful as my new dress, only better. When I wrap the scarf around

my neck, I feel almost like you've just hugged me. I can hardly wait for the real thing. Please keep yourself safe for me. With love, Jerusha."

In the spring of 1944, Sheila successfully birthed twin girls. Jerusha assisted with the delivery, a joyous experience so different from the previous year. She stayed for a couple of weeks afterward, helping Sheila adjust to two babies instead of the one she'd expected. Annie and Kerry, as the girls had been named, were happy, contented babies who seemed to flourish under the doting attention they received from their brothers.

"Our babies are the prettiest in Dawson Creek, aren't they?" Colin asked, his little chest thrust out proudly. "Did you know they're our babies, mine and Colin's, too?"

"Yes, Colin. They are pretty babies, and that's because you love them so much."

"Why does love make babies pretty, Auntie 'Rusha?" Bradley asked.

"I don't know, but it's worked with Annie and Kerry, hasn't it?"

Jerusha's second summer in Dawson Creek passed with little word from Keith and less hope of an end to the war. Christmas came again, this time without the letter she so anxiously awaited. Mrs. Sutherland's letter conveyed similar concern. *"It's been months since I've heard from our Keith. He's told me often not to worry, but in these days of unending war, I can't help myself. I try to be cheerful for the rest of my family, but I know you share my concern. Yet in spite of the worry, I feel if something had happened to him, I as his mother would know it. What a confusing mess emotions can be! I'm praying daily for his safe return and for continuing courage for you, as I trust you pray for me."*

The second anniversary of the explosion brought happy news to the Porter household. "I'm going to be a daddy!" David announced ecstatically one morning, after pounding on Jerusha's door. "My wife just told me, and I'm so thrilled I have to tell someone else. Sorry to wake you."

Jerusha laughed and hugged him, already looking forward to having a little one in the house. Maisie looked even more radiant as an expectant mother than she had as a bride. She didn't even feel nauseated in the morning, which brought out Irish indignation in Sheila.

"Sure, and it's not even fair!" she declared, her black eyes snapping. "You'll just have to pay for it with a fussy one instead of angels like my two."

Maisie just laughed and rubbed her tummy. "No, I think he'll have his daddy's happy personality."

Her only problem throughout her pregnancy was summer's heat. The least exertion caused her face to redden and her clothes to become soaked. Her feet and hands swelled. Dr. Pierce prescribed lots of rest, much to Maisie's dismay. David and Jerusha did what they could, taking her to the boardinghouse on laundry and bread-baking days to get her away from the additional heat, and preparing as many meals without cooking as possible.

Steven David Porter arrived early in the morning on September 2, causing only a little pain for his mother and an immense amount of pride for his father. Mrs. Barry came to visit the new baby, bringing with her a newspaper.

"I know those two won't be interested just yet," she whispered to Jerusha, "but I saw this headline and knew you'd want to read it." She thrust the paper at Jerusha and hurried to the bedroom.

Jerusha could barely believe her eyes. **WAR IS OVER**, the headline announced boldly. Details in the article proved it to be more than just a rumor. A tingly sense of anticipation went through her. She hadn't heard from Keith in almost a year, but neither she nor his mother had heard any bad news, either. She left the paper where David could read it if he ever took time away from his tiny son.

Steven fascinated Colin and Bradley as much as their sisters had. "He's pretty, too," Bradley observed, "but he shouldn't be 'cuz he's a boy."

"All babies are pretty, silly," Colin informed him with the immense knowledge of a youngster in his first year of school. "You'll know that when you learn to read."

Maisie regained her strength quickly. Within a couple of weeks, she was cooking again and taking the baby on daily trips to the boardinghouse. Often Jerusha spent those hours of quiet with her Bible. She'd read Psalm 91 so often she could quote it from memory, but she kept going back to read it again. *"He that dwelleth in the secret place of the most High ... "* The back door opened, but Jerusha ignored it. David had gone to the store for supplies and would holler for help if need be. She leaned her elbows on the table and continued reading. *"I will say of the Lord, he is my refuge and my fortress: my God; in him will I trust."* Strong khaki arms engulfed her in a hug from behind.

"I told you I'd come looking for you!" Keith's delighted voice growled in her ear.

She turned in his arms to look at the face she'd dreamed of countless times. He hadn't taken time to shave and looked like he hadn't slept in a week, but she thought he looked more marvelous than she'd remembered. "And I told you I'd make it easy for you to find me!" She hugged him back, hardly daring to believe she wasn't dreaming.

He kissed her with the intensity of two-and-a-half years' separation. "It took me long enough to get here. Let's not postpone our wedding any longer than we have to."

She laughed with the joy of the moment, his impatience making her feel supremely beloved. "Whatever you say, Corporal."

A Letter To Our Readers

Dear Reader:

In order that we might better contribute to your reading enjoyment, we would appreciate your taking a few minutes to respond to the following questions. When completed, please return to the following:

Rebecca Germany, Editor
Heartsong Presents
P.O. Box 719
Uhrichsville, Ohio 44683

1. Did you enjoy reading *Winding Highway*?
   ❑ Very much. I would like to see more books by this author!
   ❑ Moderately
   I would have enjoyed it more if ________________

   ____

2. Are you a member of **Heartsong Presents**? ❑Yes ❑No
   If no, where did you purchase this book? ________________

   ____

3. What influenced your decision to purchase this book? (Check those that apply.)

   ❑ Cover ❑ Back cover copy
   ❑ Title ❑ Friends
   ❑ Publicity ❑ Other________________

4. How would you rate, on a scale from 1 (poor) to 5 (superior), **Heartsong Presents'** new cover design?______

5. On a scale from 1 (poor) to 10 (superior), please rate the following elements.

___Heroine ___Plot

___Hero ___Inspirational theme

___Setting ___Secondary characters

6. What settings would you like to see covered in **Heartsong Presents** books?______________________

____

____

7. What are some inspirational themes you would like to see treated in future books?______________________

____

____

8. Would you be interested in reading other **Heartsong Presents** titles? ❑ Yes ❑ No

9. Please check your age range:
❑ Under 18 ❑ 18-24 ❑ 25-34
❑ 35-45 ❑ 46-55 ❑ Over 55

10. How many hours per week do you read? ___________

Name ______________________________________

Occupation __________________________________

Address ____________________________________

City_______________ State__________ Zip __________

Stories of Peace

by Janelle Burnham

__*River of Peace*—The remote village of Dawson Creek, British Columbia, has never had a schoolteacher before Ida Thomas. Of all her students Ida finds herself drawn to Ruth McEvan, who like Ida is struggling with a devastating family tragedy. While scorning the attentions of one man, will Ida find a man she can truly love, a man to fill her empty heart? HP100

__*Beckoning Streams*—Should Ruth McEvan remain in the familiar Peace River region and raise a family with the kind-hearted and marriage-minded Jed Spencer? The tragedy that claimed Ruth's mother and three brothers years earlier has hardened her heart. Why risk love when it can be taken away? HP119

__*Winding Highway*—No longer the elegant pastor's wife of Winnipeg, Jerusha is now taking in laundry to support herself and her brother. Yet the warmth of the townspeople in Dawson Creek and the attentions of one special army man bring Jerusha a unique sense of joy. When the war beckons, however, Jerusha must face the winding highway of life alone, perhaps forever. HP139

Send to: Heartsong Presents Reader's Service
P.O. Box 719
Uhrichsville, Ohio 44683

Please send me the items checked above. I am enclosing **$2.95 for each title** totaling $_______(please add $1.00 to cover postage and handling per order. OH add 6.25% tax. NJ add 6% tax.).

Send check or money order, no cash or C.O.D.s, please.

To place a credit card order, call 1-800-847-8270.

NAME ____________________________

ADDRESS ____________________________

CITY/STATE ____________________ ZIP __________